CW00857682

A*

A*

*   *   *

A Novel

Bret Selfman

Copyright © 2015 Bret Selfman

All rights reserved.

Cover by Michael Ellis Taylor

ISBN-13: 9781507606988
ISBN-10: 1507606982

Twitter - @Bretselfman

For my brother Jonathan

This is a work of fiction. Names, characters, businesses, places, events, and incidents are either the products of the author's imagination or used in a fictitious manner. Any resemblance to actual persons, living or dead, or actual events is purely coincidental.

‘Personality is only ripe when a man has made the truth his own.’

Søren Kierkegaard

Felixstowe—Thursday, 15 June

(In the near future)

5:00 a.m - SHANA CAPRI (19)—BEDROOM

I get in after a long, fucked-up night and go to bed.

7:00 a.m - ANDERSON MARR (17)—HOUSE

I wake up. I turn off my Sony Dream Learning Master device and do thirty minutes on my Virtual Running Track. I choose the Iceland course. I don't like the summer or the sun, and Iceland reminds me of the purity and heartening soul of a frozen winter: helps clear the mind. I break my record—three miles in thirty minutes. Then I feed the badger and let him out for a run. Then I take a shower while listening to Fearne Cotton's 'Happiness Exam A-Level Revision Champion' on my Earpad. Happiness is the one subject that I am predicted an A* in and I have to change that by getting an A** or otherwise Cornell will not accept me. I know this because of the conversation I had with the faculty advisor last Tuesday on Sony Skype.

While I am preparing my breakfast—an oatmeal egg-flap (no yoke—extra whites)—I watch the morning news report on Bloomberg and check out the latest stock news.

I need to know what is going on in the world because I am taking A-level business. I also have a small amount of money invested in Mega—a new company that deals in designer bijou holidays. It seemed like a good investment at the time and it has already made me several thousand dollars.

There is no news about Mega today although I can see that the stock has gone up a few points, which is encouraging.

I eat my egg-flap and drink some soy juice. Then I take an M and wash it down with purified rainwater. M is possibly the best thing that has come out of the GHRD (Government Health Research Department) in the last few years.

Healthniks realized five years ago that human beings actually need at least fifteen servings of vegetables and fruits a day in order to live to an optimal age. Many people tried but got ill or fed up trying to eat unrealistic amounts of food.

Fortunately, Healthcom, a Viamatic company based in Switzerland, managed to create M: a multivitamin that contains fifteen portions of vegetables and fruits.

It was very expensive but once the benefits were clear it became a must-have item. The Tories won the last election on the promise that they would be able to prescribe it on the NHS to the citizenry.

It was rumoured that Healthcom and the Tories have been financially tied together for a long time but no one has proven that. Anyhow, it has made most people happy—and now they can get their vitamin fix with a single pill. There are some who still swear off M and try to eat the full fifteen portions of organic fruit and vegetables a day but this is impractical. They call themselves Naturalists.

Healthcom has said that it plans to release pills that will substitute for meals completely. It is rumoured that this will make them a fortune from the American military industrial complex. Because of the projected financial forecast of the great return on Healthcom, I have shrewdly taken out several hundred eurocredits in shares.

Hopefully these investments will help pay my way through the six years of university that we are now expected to undertake. The education commissioner has extended the years of schooling by one year to nineteen and university to a compulsory six years in order to ease the unemployment figures.

I switch off the television, get the badger back in and put him in his room, take my packed lunch of soy rolls and vitamin water, and lock up as I leave.

As usual, I want to be at least fifteen minutes early for school—leaving a fifteen-minute margin means I can factor in all manner of unforeseen obstacles. Prompt behaviour is imperative.

7:11 a.m - CHRIS O'REILLY (18)—BEDROOM

I wake up enriched. I wash. I put on my clothes and then I walk out of the door. Today will be a good day.

7:15 a.m - RUPERT DE RICHENBACH HOFFMAN (19)—BEDROOM

I've got my window open and I'm smoking a real cigarette. It's a beautiful morning and the woods at the back of my house are looking majestic. As I puff away I listen to the morning chimes of the birds—the parakeets are drowning out the sounds of the day. Several of them are eating from the bird table. Their colours are bright and garish.

I take the last draw of death smoke from the beautiful cancerous core of the cigarette, when I see a parakeet, who is gorging from the table, get ripped apart by a sea eagle.

Its death is savage, quick, and entertaining. I finish the cigarette and try to flick it at the sea eagle but it misses and crashes into the grass. Its light is eclipsed by the shadow of the bird as it takes off with its breakfast.

The huge predator lands on the back fence and continues to maul and manhandle the carcass of the parakeet—tearing at its bright colours to reveal the fleshy bloody truth beneath.

My dog, Proust, crashes through the door and greets me good morning. His thick black hair is covered with mud from his morning walk.

I pat him on the head, light another cigarette, and settle down to some last-minute studying. I take a slurp of soya coffee, washing it back with an M. I can't fucking wait until these exams are over.

Three more long weeks of hell and then it'll all be one long beautiful summer for the rest of my life.

7:30 a.m - HEADTEACHER NICHOLAS VANDERMARK (58)—SCHOOL OFFICE

I don't know how this all started. I don't even remember why I agreed to all of it. But like a modern-day Chamberlain I did: I gave in and appeased, appeased until there was nothing left.

The school board wanted better grades—I gave them that. They wanted a healthier school—I gave it to them. They wanted proof of happy pupils—I gave it to them.

If they wanted me to bugger a Peruvian monk senseless—I'd probably do it too. I did all these things until there was nothing else left to give. The more I gave to them—the more they wanted. If you want to keep your career, then there is no alternative.

But it's never enough. Year after year, they want more. It's not enough to get good results: every year has to be better than the last and every year we have to advance up the league table a few more places. It's becoming a joke.

They went back to the A-E system ten years ago but it got inflated and so now they've created the A** grade—what next? The A*** grade or A++?! It's too much and now I've had enough, more than enough... But what to do?

Today we start the final preparations for the exams. The school must get a certain number of A** grades or else we will fail, I will be sacked, and the school will be taken over by the Government Education Trust (which is a joke considering they might as well run it anyway) and the school will be put into extraordinary measures.

So I must stay focused on the task at hand and try to ignore the other chaos going on around me: my divorce, the disciplinary hearings, my alcoholism, my prescription medication addiction, the imminent bankruptcy of the school, and my quick and worrying descent into madness. If we can get the necessary results, then all will be well.

To ensure our results, I have decided to personally intervene in the lives of the pupils. It's going to be a long horrific horrendous day...

7:31 a.m - CYNTHIA CARPATHIAN (19)—BEDROOM

I wake up and can hardly get up. My whole body aches—every single muscle and tendon feels totally spent—devoid of any life whatsoever—I don't know how I'll manage to even move about—let alone go to an exam—I just can't help feeling: what's the point?

About this and about everything—nothing really matters—not this exam, not the world, and certainly not my life. Before I had chronic fatigue syndrome, my life was great: school, studying, sports, partying, having fun.

But as soon as I developed this illness, that all slid away—having this horrible disease makes you question everything—since you've got so little energy to use, you conserve it and you really think about what's important—about what to spend this little life-force on.

And in the end it comes down to nothing—if this is what life is, then it's not worth living: not worth wearing yourself out for so long that you're a spent husk that will have to take days, weeks, months, years to recover just so that you can go through all this weariness and pain once again. What is the point?

The funny thing is, no one can really tell what chronic fatigue syndrome really is. No one knows how it's caused and whether in fact, it even exists at all.

Some think it's caused by a virus—and that the virus can be caught and there's no prevention from it. Except to me this isn't any normal virus; CFS can last for months, years, decades even. People can spend their whole lives feeling completely tired, ill, and worn out—some sick joke huh?

Others think that CFS is a made-up disease, that you don't catch it but that it's just a term used for people who are lazy or can't be bothered. This is the worst offence. The people who came up with this drivel should have the disease inflicted on them. They should be made to suffer its horror in full. They'd soon change their minds about that.

Then there is another school of thought that believes it's merely a deep depression. In other words they're saying that it's simply a condition of deep sadness—caused mentally—that causes the sufferer to lose the will to live—that saps the strength in their bodies and minds and causes this horrible existence. I can see the sense in this but I don't know how this would apply to me personally.

Was it that I just caught some virus? Or is it that I just started to think more about the world and what a messed-up horrible place it truly is? Did this cause me to get sick?

Whichever it is, all I know is that I've been thinking more about the world and more about how odious it is. It's truly a nefarious place and I want no part of it.

No matter how positive you try to be, it always comes back to this truth of horror—the horror of your own existence and the horror of the outside world.

That thought, that truly sickening horrific sensation of true reality keeps coming back again and again—and that is no way to live.

Fuck this!

I don't want to live one more day like this—and I don't think I will. What I do know is that I'm going to go back to sleep—for a long time.

8:25 a.m - SCHOOL BUS

Several youths are slumped on the long, decrepit, bendy bus in various states of despair, malaise, and drug-induced escape.

MARION: How was your weekend?

DANIEL: Shit, how was yours?

MARION: Rubbish, couldn't find my dealer, so just did a little bit of puppy and drank a couple of ciders—wasn't even enough to get a little bit of a buzz on.

DANIEL: You shouldn't mess with that shit. Don't you know that puppy is mixed with all sorts of low-grade shit?! Hey! Did you hear about Martin? Man! He got zapped!

MARION: Is he okay?

DANIEL: He's still unconscious at Ipswich Hospital. They say he's only partially brain damaged, but he won't be able to sit his exams, and with his brain damaged, the school will never let him back in—it'd ruin their grades.

MARION: When the fuck are they gonna ban zap sticks?

DANIEL: I think the government's fine with them—at least people aren't stabbing each other anymore.

MARION: Yeah, but Martin's like the third guy I know who's been zapped, and they all got brain damage. It's fucked up that people can even buy them!

DANIEL: Yup, but it's the Tory angle, dude—the zap sticks make the olds happy. It doesn't take any skill or strength to zap a gang of youths trying to rob you.

MARION: Then they should only be sold to older people.

DANIEL: Doesn't matter: you have to be twenty-five to get one but the kids can still get hold of them anywhere they want. Shit, I got mine from McMorrison's two weeks ago.

MARION: Oh, I love their McOwl burger.

DANIEL: Yeah, I know, I never thought anything that could hoot would taste sooo good!

MARION: How's your revision going? What are you predicted?

DANIEL: Mr. Chestnut says I can get an A* in biology, Miss Stephens says I could get an A** in chemistry, and Mr. Boyce says I should get an A in happiness. But unless I try harder it'll just be a B. What about you?

MARION: Predicted all A**s—but you know how that goes, the school's under a lot of pressure so they keep overinflating our predicted grades—keeps the government off their backs but I don't know if I'll even get B grades?

DANIEL: I can't handle Mondays.

Daniel takes a small wrap from his pocket and dabs his finger in it—then puts some in his mouth.

MARION: You have some dog and you didn't tell me?!

DANIEL: I've only got a little bit.

MARION: Come on, dick! Hand it over!

Daniel hands over the package; Marion looks around the bus then takes a sneaky dab. Her face lights up with instant elation.

8:30 a.m - SHANA—BEDROOM

Shana, a disaffected, upset, and pretty young lady of eighteen years, lies fast asleep in bed.

Her room is decorated like the archetypal rebellious teenager: covered in posters of bands that are designed to upset parents. From downstairs her father's voice booms out and disturbs her peaceful slumber.

FATHER: Okay, honey! Time to get up! Risey! Risey! Shineyosy!

MOTHER: It's going to be another fantastic terrific amazing happy ha-ha day for you, darling! I can just feel it!

SHANA: Fuck off!

MOTHER: Your wonderful father and I are leaving now! See you tonight, pumpkin cheeks!

SHANA: I hate you!

FATHER: Bye, my super sweety!

MOTHER: Bye, honey!

SHANA: Fuck you! I hope you both die!

Shana lights a joint. She looks savage and ready to explode with hatred.

Her gaze turns to look at the posters of Arthur Scargill, Che Guevara, Hugo Chavez, and a neo-punk group called the New Militants she has adorning her walls. Shana lights her joint, takes a big toke, and blows it out.

SHANA: Fucking capitalists—I hope they crash their fucking Tory car.

On their way to work at the local party headquarters, the Mathesons discuss their wayward daughter.

FATHER: Shana seemed happy this morning.

MOTHER: Yes, I'm glad that she's up and about. She seems back to her normal, super self.

FATHER: Yup—chipper and hipper.

MOTHER: I thought it was just a fad she was going through.

FATHER: And she's all over it now.

MOTHER: Gone and done with.

FATHER: She's been there and done that.

MOTHER: She just needed to get through it on her own.

FATHER: She saw the light at the end of the tunnel.

MOTHER: I knew she'd come through it.

FATHER: She never needed therapy. She was just—what's that word—begins with an R?

MOTHER: Retreating.

FATHER: No, not that, it's another R word.

MOTHER: Reverberating.

FATHER: No, it's reb—something.

MOTHER: Reblon?

FATHER: No, that's a clothing company I think. No, it's rebelling, that's it!

MOTHER: Of course that's it—she was just rebelling! That's what she was doing!

FATHER: That's the one.

MOTHER: And now it's all going to be nothing but fun.

FATHER: Fun in the sun.

MOTHER: Of course, it's June.

FATHER: No moon in June.

MOTHER: No moon now but probably soon.

FATHER: You know these new pills that Doctor Johnson has got us on are great—I think they're really working.

MOTHER: Yup, yes indeed, I really think the gloom has run away and won't be back for another day.

FATHER: It's gone on a happy gay holiday.

MOTHER: Packed its bags and gone to Chad.

FATHER: And now I'm no longer mad.

MOTHER: And I'm glad.

FATHER: And that's no fad!

MOTHER: Happy that we decided to stay together?

FATHER: Happy indeed. You know, I knew once we put Shana on those pills that it would bring her out of it.

MOTHER: Works for me.

FATHER: As for me—Hee hee!

In Shana's bedroom she is pouring a jar of pills down the sink.

SHANA: Tory capitalist drug-happy fuckheads.

Shana's phone rings.

SHANA: Hello...What?! No! I don't know whether I'm going into school today? Because I don't know whether I can deal with their bullshit fascistic prescriptive farcical nonsense! Bastard school capitalist wankers...Yeah, I know it's a means to an end—but still...Yeah, whatever...Yeah, see you later...Fuckhead!

Shana takes an air pistol that she has stashed under her bed and starts shooting a poster of a rotund and ageing Ed Balls.

SHANA: Die, you puffed-up fat piece of shit.

(SHANA'S THOUGHTS): I lay back on my bed and I look up at my ceiling and I'm thinking: I hate this ceiling. I've always hated ceilings—they're limiting, just like walls—they're there to keep you prisoner—keep you stifled—keep you from being free—keep you suppressed—just another instrument of the state—they're just there to show you your place—to say—right! You stay there—you don't cause any trouble—make sure you don't ever come out again. I fucking hate Tory capitalist fucking ceilings. One day I'll live out in the wild... I hate everybody and everything.

8:34 a.m - ARNOLD RAVEN—FELIXSTOWE TOWN CENTRE

Seventeen, pale and wiry, Arnold is a high-school dropout. He is walking along the streets—kicking at bits of garbage.

He takes out a small black book full of his poems and he raps along to one entitled 'A-LEVEL DROPOUT' as he moves along the street.

'I buy a juice from the store and walk some more
Can't stand this fucking place—I'm sore.
Everyone can go to hell
It's not for me to go out and sell
My soul to a stupid-ass school bell
It can ring-ring on time
Everybody else's future it can chime
But not for me no more
I'd rather sleep on a dusty floor.
That sickening death of the soul can stay
In its place while I go play.
The bureaucrats can sing and deliver figures on a whim
I know the fucking score
That's why I'm not at that shit-dump anymore.'

Arnold Raven walks further along the street until he gets to the Spa Pavilion Gardens.

Here lies a beautiful series of benches, bushes, and flowers. It's also home to numerous drug dealers who peddle the popular modern substance of choice: dog. It's a potent purple powder made from mixing a Korean dog tranquiliser with cocaine.

Arnold locates his dealer among a series of innocuous individuals pretending to walk dogs and approaches him with his money ready.

8:45 a.m - SCHOOL GATES

The school gates—tall, thick, and seemingly impenetrable—open up. The queuing school buses proceed inside—screened on either side by security officers wielding large zap sticks. One of these, Brian O'Daniels, mutters to himself, 'I hate my job, I hate these kids, and I hate everything.'

9:00 a.m - SOMEONE SOMEWHERE

Someone once told me that school was like prison—you just had to do your time as peacefully and as purposefully as you can. But just like prison, sometimes you can end up getting buggered senseless.

9:03 a.m - ANDERSON MARR—BUSINESS CLASS

I'm taking notes with my audometer and iPalm in Mr. Krasinsky's business development class. The case study is about the burgeoning success of the American weapons manufacturer Dayglow.

He's recounting how by starting lots of small little insurrections, coups, and other such outbreaks of conflict across the world through surrogates, mercenaries, and puppet leaders, the American industrial complex was able to keep everybody fighting—the Asian Bloc (Pakistan, Afghanistan, Iraq, Iran), the Russian Confederation, Anglo-America, India-China, etc...The arms race has reached new and severely profitable levels—tempered by the fact that defence systems have now made nuclear weapons obsolete. This means that for the first time in almost a century, wars in the future can be fought on a huge scale with large armies.

While Mr. Krasinsky hands out Dayglow badges, weblinks, and free music downloads from their website (Dayglow sponsors this section of the course), I take the opportunity to check my bio-readings on my body-monitor—resting heart rate down to sixty—good, that means that the new ultra low-fat and zero-sodium diet I'm on is having the desired effect—liver functions at an optimum level, brain matter in tip-top shape, muscle-growth steady, waist at thirty inches—good, all is acceptable and the matter of the lower heart rate is a pleasing bonus.

Mr. Krasinsky lands the 'Hi from Dayglow!' package on my desk station and wishes me all the best for the scholarship to Princeton. I make some inane conversation with him—reassuring him of his investment—creating a connection—and he moves on—while he goes around delivering the rest of the packages to the rest of my classmates, I check my appointment card for the rest of the day:

12:30 p.m.	Lunch and check Bloomberg stocks.
1:30 p.m.	Chemistry.
2:30 p.m.	Information systems class.
3:30 p.m.	Optional revision session.
5:00 p.m.	Workout.
6:30 p.m.	Mind-embellishment.
7:30 p.m.	Low-sodium low-fat meal.
8:00 p.m.	Final revision.
10:00 p.m.	Enhanced meditation.
11:00 p.m.	Sleep slot.

Perfect: this is exactly the programme I need to make sure I am on course for tomorrow's examinations.

<u>9:05 a.m - ANGELES MONTAINE CATHCART-FARQUAR (18)</u>

Angeles, rich, beautiful, glamorous, and supercilious, pulls up to school in her chauffeured limousine.

ANGELES: So I arrive at school post-fashionably late because I made my driver wait. I can't believe I have been at this school for so long—it's really beginning to become a pain. But I am happy because I'm wearing my new Yves Saint Laurent dress and my pink vintage Manolo heels. I am listening to my iLobe—I don't know who the songs are by and I don't care because it isn't very good—it's a mix that Marco did for me—various bits of post-pop, neo-pop, post-metallic thrash rockabilly, pre-gothic grime, and old progressive witch house.

I dumped Marco three months ago but still he buzzes and hovers around me, constantly trying to get in my pussy, doing anything and everything to try and win me over—he doesn't stop. Marco has a certain machoistic charm but I am more than over him now. I need someone with style and a big bank account—although it's not like I'm poor—my parents own one of the biggest and most exclusive houses along the cliff-tops.

What else can I tell you? Well, I suppose I'm quite like those new-traditionalists when it comes to my beliefs and that includes preserving my dignity. I do not intend to have intercourse until after a year of dating; so far, only one man has met that challenge.

My future plans: well, the idiots at this school have not seen fit to predict me good grades! That's for sure! In fact, they have predicted me awful results: all B grades! Even my influential parents' intervention has not caused the school to change them. My teachers said they were being over-optimistic with the B grade predictions as it was! What is the world coming to?! Well, because of that, I will not go to an American university. But then again, I never wanted to.

Instead, my parents have promised to fund my foray into London where I will work in fashion and eventually set up my own label. I know that people say that London is so 1990s and that it is over—that nobody in their right mind should go there anymore but that's exactly why I'm going there—to help revitalise it—the capital needs people like me.

I'm walking to my first class when I see that bitch, Shana Capri. 'Hi, Shana, you absolute bitch—how are you?' I say in my mind. She sees me and sticks her fingers up.

'Fuck a finger, Angeles, you skanky slut sack of shit.'

I have more dignity than to reply to such comedy—'Skank!?'—who does she think she is?! She's the skankiest girl I've ever met! What absolute irony!

Angeles...I like my name. My parents named me so because they conceived me in Los Angeles. I have been there once—a nice place—bit crowded though and too many ethnics, if you know what I mean.

I'm in the science corridor—it stinks of horrible science smells in here—awful, my nose should not have to tolerate such impurities. Mr. Backthwaite passes me and tells me that my assignment is late, then he wishes me luck in my exams. I find that highly amusing as I don't even take any classes with him! I apologise to him and tell him that I will get the assignment in very soon.

I enter my humanities revision class and Mr. Rapp has already started his 4D Powerpoint Plus on the Third Gulf War (the one with Yemen I think).

I sit at the back and take out my iPalm. I go Superline and check my Mugbook—no new updates but then again I only checked it five minutes ago. I decide to make a post: 'I'm sitting in my humanities revision class listening to Mr. Rapp's crash revision on the Third Gulf War and I'm fucking bored.'

I look over the photos that were posted of me from Amy Satchell-Power-Thomas's birthday at the Golden Panda last week—I look cute. Amy looks awful but I feel obliged to make a nice comment so I post under her picture: 'You look supercute in your Prada dress, girl!' Then I decide to be funny, so where there is a picture of her with a Chinese waiter I comment, 'So when's the wedding?'

The funny thing is that Amy does have a thing about Chinese guys—she's the best in her class at Mandarin and she's been over there on an exchange trip. She's even thinking of going over there for university—which is crazy as she's good enough to go to any institution in the states.

Amy's probably my best friend—although recently I've been spending a lot of time with Warp Hindrance-Thomas. She's a new girl who used to live in London—if she doesn't get into Cornell—and they've recently tightened up their exams so she won't, then we will go to London and share a loft together which should be a lot of fun! Warp drinks a lot but it's cute—I've been there and done that with alcohol—but never any drugs, never with the drugs—drugs are for total losers—every second person at this school seems to be hooked on dog.

I mean, please?! I would never do something that was named after such a silly animal.

I smoke but they are only E-ettes—proven to be harmless and I inhale the more expensive ones that are less damaging to your health. I inhale because I enjoy it but also because I've noticed that a lot of the fashion world enjoys

E-ettes and that if you don't, you are almost outcast—so, for professional reasons, I inhale.

I check the Mugbook updates again—Rudolphio Match-Rees has posted up something about a pillow party at his tonight. Pillow parties are more or less orgies—you bring your pillow, put it in a room with all the other pillows, and then at some point you all go in there and you fuck everyone else. How juvenile! I got all that out of the way by the age of fifteen.

Rudolphio's a slease anyway but a very good soccer player, and people tell me he could go professional—that he could possibly be good enough to play in the MLS. I just hope he doesn't get any dodgy diseases! Shit, he will if that skank slut whore Shana Capri goes!

What really ticks me off is that my parents and Shana's parents are friends and we have to tolerate each other at our parents' parties.

We used to get on when we were very young but that was a long time ago.

I respond to Rudolphio's post and tell him that I will not be attending. Then the moment takes me and I cannot resist—I post up: 'Shana Capri is a skanky whore crab-infested bitch-head who shits herself.' Ha! The act of writing it pleases me but I know that it will be disadvantageous to leave it up so I delete it.

The 4D Powerpoint Plus has ended and Mr. Rapp is ranting on about the importance of using quotes from Mitchell Rayworth's textbook to back up our arguments. Then he goes into a sermon on how lucky we are to have the answers given to us and that all we need to do is memorise the answers and regurgitate them on paper. Then he goes down memory lane and says about how, back in his day, the students went into exams not knowing what the exam questions would be?! Whatever, Mr. Rapp.

<u>9:07 a.m - DR. JEFFERSON—ST. CLEMENT'S MENTAL ASSISTANCE ASYLUM</u>

The patient Harrison Lemont-Daniels is in a catatonic state—the result of which is his overdosing on the illegal learning drugs A* and NL (Next Level). The patient stirs every so often to scream and blurts out a series of incomprehensible words and occasionally he makes partial sense and he seems to be trying to communicate about the subjects he was revising for and the universities he had applied to…

HARRISON: Yale, Brown, La Crosse—Will Self, subfunctionalist, wizzle berries! Murrfffff!!!! Wizzzzlaaaa! Murfff! Gonnnnaa yuckatab gunnar yuckatabbbyyyyyyyyyyyyyyyyyy!

9:08 a.m - DNA MATLOCK—ADVANCED MATHEMATICS CLASS

I'm sitting in advanced mathematics class and I'm pondering the Chinese apocalypse. When will it be? The strange Chinese alien woman who sometimes visits me at night says that there will be no forewarning, but at the last minute she will appear and beckon me to follow her and that I will be all right and I will be saved.

There doesn't appear to be any lasting friction between the West and China right now, so I wonder when this will occur? The West has more or less given into China's economic, financial, and corporate dominance as they don't fear the Chinese in a military capacity as it will clearly be mutually assured destruction if it comes to war.

Barney 'Krispy Kreme' Tuckworth is trying to answer a question on quantum mechanics that Mr. Lu is providing, but his fat frame can't quite process the equation. Barney is one of the only obese people I know who has been given corporate sponsorship, but then again the guy's a walking advert for donut consumption—and particularly for cronuts—(the croissant-donut mélange). There isn't an hour goes by without him shoveling some fried sugary snack into his quite estimable gob.

He's also a popular guy—the big loveable lummox who's always full of warmth and glee—the perfect promotion for the benefits of donut consumption being that if you eat these donuts, then you'll be happy, funny, warm, and loved too—I figure that's why they opted for Barney. It's clever capitalism.

Mr. Lu is losing patience as Barney continues to struggle. Barney suddenly says, 'Don't have a clue, sir, but would you like a cronut?' The class erupts into laughter and Mr. Lu breaks into a wide smile and pats him on the head. Barney's chubby face glows with fatty satisfaction.

9:12 a.m - RUPERT DE RICHENBACH HOFFMAN—TOILETS

I'm in the University Prep block toilets and I'm late for my first class. There's no way I can face my lesson without a hit so I've come here to do a quick bump of dog.

I wipe the toilet seat with anti-bac tissues—making sure it's clean—then I take the capsule that I purchased this morning for thirty eurocredits from my dealer down the gardens and sprinkle the purple powder on the toilet seat. It looks pure. I don't know why dog is purple. Apparently it's something about the chemical reaction when the dog tranquiliser mixes with the cocaine. I don't know anybody who does normal cocaine any more—even the stars have switched over to dog. Michael Rodgers—the winner of last year's *SCPG (Simon Cowell's Pop God*) was caught recently with three grammes of it. It looked like it was all over for him, but he went on *Simon and Sonia's Chat Factory* and made a big apology to his fans—it could go either way for him now.

I can't stand Rodgers or what he represents—what I do care about is dog. At least Michael Rodgers and I have that in common. The thing I like about dog is that it gives you a smooth high that allows you to get on with your life without too harsh of a comedown. One bump will last you from one to three hours, which means you can sustain the high.

There are no tell-tale signs of mild dog use: no red eyes, no twitching, gurning, etc…It's only the heavy users that you can immediately tell: their skin has gone purple and their pupils have retracted to a small dot. They shuffle around like zombies. A boy at the school got to this point just before Christmas, I hear that his parents sent him off to rehab but he couldn't stick it. Once you turn purple it's permanent—you're stigmatised. The last thing I heard was that he was walking the streets of London, selling himself for dog. I wonder who would want to sleep with someone purple? Prince maybe?

I'm never going to let dog get control of me—I only use a few times a day and after the exams I'm quitting—well, at least until I sit my university entrance exams—you see, dog helps you focus on your studies. I chop up the powder with my Santander eurocard. It's the best card to chop up the powder as it's got the sharpest edge. It falls apart nicely, smoothly, and I sweep up the powder into two fine lines. I take a twenty eurocredit from my wallet and send the powder up one nostril then the next...Yes! The effect is immediate, this is just as good—if not better than the last batch.

Now I'm ready for class. I dab the last of the powder with my hand and walk out of the cubicle.

9:45 a.m - SHANA—ENGLISH CLASSROOM

I am pretending to listen to the English lecture whilst listening to my Earpod:

Today's Playlist:

1: New Militants: 'Eat Your Earpod'
2: Bad Bastardz: 'Fucking Up the Underground'
3: Sad Kate: 'Your Mum's Dead'
4: New Militants: 'Apples and Pears'
5: The Jam: 'Eton Rifles'
6: NWA: 'Fuck the Police'
7: Jack White: 'Yellow Belly Blues'
8: New Militants: 'Smack You Right the Fuck Up'
9: Jeremy Cadaver: 'You Are Not Alive'
10: Sad Kate: 'Bite Your Dick Off'
11: Sad Kate: 'I'm Gonna Do Your Mum Up the Bum'

9:50 a.m - MR. DEWBERRY (HEAD OF ENGLISH)—STAFFROOM

I come into the staffroom after having had a sneaky E-ette and immediately go over to the electronic whiteboard to read all the day's directives from the morning briefing.

1) Exams start tomorrow so keep reminding students to be positive.
2) All staff should be available until at least 10:00 p.m. tonight to help with last-minute strategic revision.
3) Postings are up for staff obliged to supervise the overnight revision and instruction on the camp-bed guard duty rota. Sedatives are to be judiciously dispensed to overanxious overnight students.
4) Local and national press have been hammering us about spoon-feeding students exam answers—don't talk to the press. If pushed, then just remind them that the 'Exam Laptop Online System' didn't work and that we operate a 'Golden Honour System.'
5) Students aren't smiling enough! They must start smiling! A reminder that if Ofsted comes in and assesses us for happiness we will fail. All pupils should be smiling for at least 75 percent of the day. Remind them that they are continuously assessed on happiness and will fail if they are not looking content or joyful.
6) Duty teams to check toilets more regularly—dog use is on the rise; police may do spot checks. The last thing we need is more purple students! The media had a field day with the last ones.
7) Robert Martinez's dad died last night—TLC please—he is an A* student and he must sit his exams and pass them successfully—we can't afford to lose him.
8) Applicants for the new happiness coordinator are coming in tomorrow afternoon—Steve and Nimbit will handle interviews.

Just another day of absolute bullshit then...

<u>10:00 a.m - VANDERMARK—(58)—IN HIS OFFICE, STARING OUT OF HIS WINDOW</u>

I don't know how much longer I want to stay alive. This world has gone mad and I no longer want to live in it. These notes will hopefully make people in the future understand why I no longer want to be here.

The ridiculous pressures of this job are one of the first reasons. Staffing levels are critical. When the Tories made drastic cuts in education, they also dropped salary levels for teachers and university professors so fewer people wanted to enter the profession; so then the government made it easier to become a teacher. They dropped the qualifications necessary to be an educator to a ridiculously low level—then parents complained about the lack of quality teaching so the government gave 'power to the parents' to sack teachers—which led to staff shortages—which led to an impact on academic outcomes—a vicious circle.

So now, more than ever, we are under pressure to get results. So we inflate grades and spoon-feed the kids the exam questions. There is no other option if we are to get improved results year-on-year.

On top of that: a shocking wave of violence has spread among the young. There are numerous theories surrounding this. Some say that it's a by-product of the electromagnetic charges that come from mobile phones and computers while others say it's the gradual abandonment of parental responsibility. Whatever it is, it makes life a lot harder.

Drug dealing, stabbing, gang-related crime, and general high-level disruption are now rife. Recently the pupils have also been using zap sticks in their altercations. Our school has certain factions that are involved in violent gang activity against our local rivals: the 'Well-Done Academy.'

We can't even rely on the police for help. The Tories' huge cuts in taxes may have helped many families financially but it's meant drastic cuts in policing so there are fewer boots on the streets.

The Tories' ideology of the 'New Society', where we police ourselves and look after ourselves, is a complete failure. Perhaps to detract from their failures, the Tories have now developed the 'Happy Society'—a series of ridiculous policies that are designed to bring happiness into the lives of us all. Our part in this is to teach the pupils to be *happy*!

So we have been tasked with introducing the happiness curriculum and we are judged to be a failing school if we fail to deliver this correctly!

This has infiltrated into the media too—as the government's happiness champion, Christopher Biggins, has been given considerable powers. So now all television channels must dedicate half their time to positivity- and happiness-based programming and the news channels and newspapers must also find happy and positive news stories to share with their audience in at least 50 percent of their coverage.

The BBC had to create a head of delivering happiness post. This person—I think it's currently Andy Peters—launched some revolutionary changes.

Research showed them that *Eastenders* was causing depression in many people so they cut it and launched *Westenders* instead. It shows the blissful side of life in the West End of London—storylines are upbeat and always leave on a happy note that has to be matched by never-ending highs of life fulfilment. The cast is always getting married, getting promoted, winning the lottery, succeeding in their hobbies, forming new friendships. Surprisingly it's the BBC's most popular show of the moment.

The Tories are convinced that if they keep telling everyone that they are happy, then this will be enough. It's all part of 'The Big Smile,' they call it.

The government's desire to save money has meant that it has let commercial companies take over academies and allowed them to teach their own curriculums. Pupils at these schools are indoctrinated with corporate beliefs and work practices and are trained up to be part of their workforce. Some are little more than glorified sweatshops. I hear that the SKY Television Academy in Ipswich has its students do its market research and man help-lines.

This is modern education.

10:01 a.m - MARTHA TRUEBERRY (19)—BY THE LOCKERS

My name is Martha but many people call me 'Chocolate Box.' They call me that because I eat a lot of chocolate a lot of the time. When I'm not at school, I volunteer for the RSPCA. When I am at school, I spend a lot of time eating chocolate out of my box. I keep my box in my locker, and when I get the chance I like to eat everything that is in the box. My favourite chocolate is all of it. I don't eat dinner because I'm not hungry after I've eaten everything in my chocolate box.

10:05 a.m - SIGMUND HAUSER—ENGLISH LITERATURE

I'm sitting in English—listening to the 4D version of Conrad's *Heart of Darkness*—while I stare at Shana. She looks gorgeous today—to me she looks like a young Lindsey Lohan—long tussled strawberry-blond hair—she's five-ten with a fiery tenacious attitude to match her fierce stare. She's wearing a short red skirt so you can see her long luscious legs; she has a New Militants t-shirt on—a neogothic rockabilly anarchist group who recently staged a concert near Ed Ball's country estate before they were arrested and charged with the 2021 Blanket Terrorism Act. Her black bag has a load of other groups white-lined onto it: 'All Teddy Bears Must Die,' 'The Die! Tories! Die! 4' and 'Marvin Haggler Ate My Dad.' She listens intensely as she makes notes on her iPalm. She notices me staring and looks up at me in fury. I look around at the rest of the classroom: it's a small group, only eight other students—we're the top set apparently.

We are the chosen ones—the ones that have been streamlined into the so-called A** set—and if we all get A**, then the school will be on course and the English department will have scored the necessary 25 percent of A** required.

I don't know if my peers know, but I'm fully aware that I am part of a machine—just a cog in the engine—that we are all in a play and that I have a part to engage in just like all the others—and I'm also fully aware that our teachers are spoon-feeding us—giving us the answers and prompting us on how to answer the questions that will come up on the exam sheet.

Lessons were getting more interesting a few years back when England started embracing the Danish system of enquiry-based questions that needed to use the SuperNet to research. Laptops were set up in exam halls and students were trusted not to cheat—nobody figured that they would—or then again, maybe that's what was hoped they'd do. Anyway, the inevitable happened and the government lost all the data for a whole year's worth of results for A-levels—and every single student had to re-sit their exams. There was outrage and parent pressure meant that we all went back to the old ways of sitting examinations. The perpetrators were never caught. Some say it was a careless Whitehall technocrat and others say that it was a group of gifted computer-literate disgruntled students who had been expelled from their school and who hacked in and wiped the lot. Whatever the case, it just means I and my fellow peers now have to sit through two years of spoon-feeding to get our tickets to university and the wider world.

10:15 a.m - ANGELES—MEDIA STUDIES CLASS

So I'm in media studies revision class and I'm going through my Mugbook contacts, deciding who to keep and who to delete—I do it every now and again. I consider it my spring cleaning. I get to Melissa Wintour—the adopted daughter of a famous fashion mogul—she will be useful in the future—I often go up and visit her in London and she will more than help my cause when I want to progress.

I get rid of a few deadbeats and retards and then I'm good. I go back to listening to the teacher. There is the usual spiel about the importance of citing your references—of making sure that this theory and that theory are considered and making sure that all the prepared answers that we have been memorising are regurgitated.

Mr. Habbord is youngish and attractive—I used to have a crush on him but I grew out of it. He always gives me good marks so I've got no need to flirt or work my feminine ways with him.

10:17 a.m - DNA MATLOCK—MATHS CORRIDOR

This school is a crumbling block of decaying horseshit.

10:23 a.m - TERESA YOUNG-LEARSTEIN (18)—HEALTH AND WELFARE CLASS

I'm listening to our guidance-enabler rabbit on about how it is up to us to make the world a better place; about how our freedom and happiness is our own choice; about how we have to recognise the power of now; about how we have to own our joy—at one point she stops and seems to have run out of government bullshit but then she remembers some more and keeps banging on—going on about our ability to 'feel fear or fun'—top marks for alliteration, Miss!

The bullshit positivity-talk indoctrination never changes. For the last five years I have had to listen to this scheisse every single morning.

I scan the room and immediately Chris O'Reilly's gaze meets mine. Chris is probably the second most handsome person in this class (in a strange sort of way) but is easily the most intelligent. Every word that comes from Miss Markwhich is met with a condescending grin and nod from him—Chris is the leader of the Black Hatters—a gang who wear bizarre hats: trilbies, yarmulkes, babushkas, etc...Chris wears a tall black hat. He has been leader of the Black Hatters for a year and a half—ever since Oppenheimer Harris was killed in a fight with the Warthogs.

Allegedly, many people think that Chris was the one who killed Oppenheimer. The Warthogs are a gang from the Well-Done Academy—the only other academy in our town.

The two gangs fight regularly. Nobody really remembers why it started or why it continues. Some think it's due to boredom and others to inherited aggression. This is a theory that the reason why we young people are so aggressive today is due to all the radioactivity and 'negative waves' from overusing mobile phones and electric devices that flooded our parents' bodies in the 1990s and early 2000s.

Anyway, the gangs tangle over territory, school-pride, and dog-dealing. The Hatters are heavy users and anybody who knows the score knows not to buy off them as they have the worst watered-down stuff—no chance of going purple with their crap.

10:29 a.m - ANGELES—CLASSROOM

I'm taking a quick look at the new '*HM and Gabbana*' web page. This season's new rages include jazz-pants—jeans that have crazy patchwork colours and patterns on them—they could be fun and cute for a while—but you can't really be serious about something so dumb for very long.

Then there's armslengths—which are shirts that shrink to exactly the size of your arms—robotic fabric that measures how big you are and grow accordingly—great for young people with still-developing bodies—the robotic tissue market's gonna work really well for them—then there's the ARB—which is of course bra spelt backward—the arb is described as an inside-out bra—which a lot of celebs have endorsed.

For men, there's the dilby—a variant on the trilby, which was in last season—but mostly, hats are definitely out and someone should probably tell that to Chris O'Reilly and the dumb-hatters.

Green was supposed to be the in-colour for the summer—a sort of 'get back to nature' style thing—but that's passed and not been very successful. Yellow is going to be the thing that really takes off this season.

The biggest new trend is laser-coloured vaginas, as now you can colour your pussy—it's a radical and progressive idea.

I'm looking through the *New Young Lady* magazine: it has an interview with Fearne Cotton Jr.—what makes her tick? I skim through that and go to the interview with Charles Chutney—then, 'Tips on how to make your vag look smaller,' 'Tips on how to make your tits look bigger,' an interview with a famous fluffer, 'Ten ways to make your man smile,' 'Ten ways to make your man cry,' 'Carrots—nature's superfood,' 'The royal family: should we have them back again?'—an interview with the last king to ever rule England—King William. I flick to this and scan through the article. I like the idea of the royal family—I was too young to remember when we got rid of them—must've been when I was six or seven—they were just suddenly thrown out and all their assets were stripped—except for their house in Norfolk where some of them still live. Now Buckingham Palace is hired out as a hotel/tourist attraction/concert hall—the ex-King William says he's happy living a normal family life with Kate who has a successful business—says he's still very busy with various charities and engagements and that he likes his new life.

10:30 a.m - JASPER JODPHURS-SMITH (18)—AT HOME

I'm bunking off school today because the only exam I've got for the next few days is the happiness exam and I don't need to revise for that bullshit. Instead, I'm staying home because the latest game for the Ninsega came out: *Battle for Saturn*—it's where you take command of a death ranger and have to exterminate the sky goblins who have ransacked the earth colony on Saturn. The game is in 4D and my immersion goggles came today with the new nasal interface. It's gnarly because when you blast the goblins, their blood and guts explode everywhere, and you can smell their burnt flesh, which smells sort of like what rotten meat would I guess. If you go right up to a dead goblin and blast its head, you can scoop up bits of brain and inhale it—it's gross, like rotten turds. A lot of people have been known to throw up and the game comes with a health warning because of this. I can't wait for the taste interface—should be rad.

Just recently, games have been getting really cool. I'm not into the sex ones—although I know some of my friends get into the *Porno Master* games where you play a porn actor and have to fuck your way through a series of films to get to the final orgy scene—there's a penis interface, which mimics the act of a blowjob and humping, with different tightness levels depending on the girl. A special vacuum and container cleans up your cum. I don't know any of my friends who've gotten to the final orgy scene—they all blow their loads when they have to face Jennifer Young. I'm scared of the porn games because the guys I know who play them have gone a bit weird and spend way too much time on them. Maybe I'll try it over the summer—but then again, there are a lot of games coming out this year and I won't have time for all of them. *Torture Death Chamber*, where you score points by kidnapping and torturing tourists in different cities, is top of my list. I've played the bootleg and it's way far-out.

Ninsega have promised that next year they'll be releasing a taste interface add-on. Errr, can you imagine what will happen with the porn games? You'll probably be able to taste pussy—well, if it's Jennifer Young that might not be a bad idea!

My iPalm messaging system flashes up. It's a message from Dad: 'Go to school, dickhead! You've got a revision class.'

Shit—I guess the goblins of Saturn are safe again for the rest of today. I save my game and get ready for school. Happiness revision class...Oh joy.

10:33 a.m - DOCTOR—ST. CLEMENTS HOSPITAL

Harrison is being restrained—despite the sedatives he is on, he woke up and went berserk. He tried to access the hospital's laptop room—claiming he had to revise for his 'Weee willy weebil wilt'—then started foaming at the mouth and kept repeating: 'Yuckateeeeeebbeeeeeeeeeeee yuckateeebeeeeeeeeeeee! Yuckavttteeebeeeeeeeeeeeeeet!!!!'

I prescribe him a stronger batch of sedatives and a course of anti-psychotic pills.

<u>10:35 a.m - ANDERSON MARR—MATHS CORRIDOR</u>

I'm walking along the corridor when I spy an individual I believe to be called Rupert. I adjust my gaze to meet his but he averts my looks and even seems to make an effort to avoid my physical proximity—fascinating, what has caused this consternation in him?

<u>10:45 a.m - RUPERT AND SHANA—BY THE 'SUPERBIKE' SHEDS</u>

I'm having a cheeky 'real cigarette' behind the bike sheds with a couple of randoms I don't know. Nobody really smokes proper cigarettes anymore; they all smoke those horrible E-ettes. The fines you can get for smoking real cigarettes puts most people off smoking them now. I got these: Davidoff Blacks, from some guy down the Spa Gardens—they're not bad—from Germany—where they still smoke proper cigarettes.

'Room for another?'

It's Shana and she's looking good—I used to date Shana—last year in fact, we had some wild times—she's great in bed—but also as crazy as a box of soaped-up salamanders. I couldn't keep up with her mood swings so it had to end.

'Thought you were never coming to school again?'

'Move over, dick.'

Shana takes out a pack of Playboy cigarettes and lights one up with her Walther PPK lighter—stylish, I've always liked that one a lot. Tried to steal it from her once.

I always liked the way she smoked her cigarettes too—she sucks on them hard and lustrously—her mouth really engorging the cigarette—you can kind of picture in your mind's eye what she might be thinking about when she does that.

'You didn't answer my question, Shana. Why are you here? What happened to 'Fuck Vandermark! Fuck the school! And fuck my parents!?'

'I had a better idea—I'm gonna finish school, go to Wisconsin, sit the entrance exams, pass, start school there, and then I'm gonna blow it the fuck up—the ultimate act of fuck-you to the stupid fucking school system and the ultimate fuck-you to the stupid fucking ideals of my deadhead, happed-up, fucked-up parents.'

'How'd you get the grades to apply to Wisconsin?' asks one of the randoms.

'Do you really think you'll get away with it? The agents profile everyone going there now—they'll be on you all the time—they keep tabs on girls like you.'

'Duhhhhh, Rupert! I'll be a good girl for a few years—then when the time is right—kaboom.'

'You using dog again? Is that why you're talking this way? You got any?'

'No, I'm done with that shit—just the Mary Jane for me now.'

'You going to Warp's study party?'

'Don't know—maybe, we'll see.'

'Seriously though? How'd you get the grades to apply to Wisconsin—I couldn't even get a callback to Columbia!' chimes Random 2.

Random 1 says, 'Saw the new Simon Amstell movie last night—very funny.'

RANDOM 2: He's a twat.

RANDOM 1: Seriously, it's good—he plays a beggar who steals a car and because it's this secret agent's car and he looks like him, they all think it's him, and so he has to live this double secret life.

RANDOM 2 (Sarcastically): Sounds amazing.

RANDOM 1 (To Shana): What were your predicted grades then?

RUPERT (To Shana): What are you doing at the weekend?

SHANA: Fantasizing about killing my parents—maybe actually doing it.

RANDOM 1 (To Random 2): What about you, man? Where have you got your preliminaries?

RANDOM 1: Ahh mate, I couldn't even get through to the next round with a Yank uni—the only ones that would take me were English and Dutch colleges.

RANDOM 2: Shit, mate, sorry. You're fucked then.

RANDOM 2: My fault. I was fucked up on dog for most of last year—I'm lucky to still be here.

RUPERT: Well, me and some of the others are going up to London for a mid-exam party day—you up for it?

SHANA: I already told you, I'm killing my parents this weekend.

RUPERT: Well, if you change your mind—just let me know.

RANDOM 1 (To Shana): Are you on Mugbook? I'll add you.

SHANA (To Rupert): Did you know that the BNP are campaigning in this town? How has it come to this?

RUPERT: We're gonna get the A-train up—only takes sixty minutes now—so we'll go early on Saturday and have the whole day—we're thinking a bit of shopping in Soho, then a bar brawl crawl in Clapham and back on the last train, whattayou think?

SHANA: Maybe I'll blow up the BNP headquarters.

RANDOM 1 (To Shana): My Mugbook is JIMJUGGLER—just search and add me.

RANDOM 2 (To Random 1): I'll see you later, mate. I've gotta go to Mandarin class.

RUPERT (To Shana): There's quite a wild crowd going: Warp, Vanessa, Simone, Truck, Cressida—Oh, sorry, I mean YouTube—still can't believe she changed her name—seems like everyone's selling out now.

SHANA: I've gotta blow something up soon or I'll go crazy.

RANDOM 1: I used to be on YourSpace but it got so full of Head commercials it was doing my head in. I don't mind paying the Mugbook subscription as long as they don't start downloading shit adverts about Wilson's washing powder and McMorrison's into my head—that can't be good for you can it?

RUPERT: I heard Cressida was offered a full university scholarship from YouTube for her name change and a hundred-eurocredit-a-week bursary. I guess it really is true what they've been saying. If you're attractive, clever, and good at sports, you can pay your way through uni with these dumb name-change deals. Look at Tommy changing his name to 'Subway' and Nigel with 'Mars Bar.' Well, at least Mars Bar is quite a cool name actually. But me? No, I'd never do it. (Rupert flicks his cigarette into the hedge over the other side of the fence.) What about you Shana? If the New Militants asked you to change your name, would you?

SHANA: I hate my life.

RANDOM 1: The thing I like about Mugbook is the access panel—it's slick, sleek, smooth, modern—it works.

RUPERT: So you gonna come then?

SHANA: What?

RUPERT: On Saturday, to the midway exam party?

SHANA: I don't know what the fuck you're talking about.

RANDOM 1 (To Shana): So, what is your Mugbook address?

Shana throws down her cigarette and storms off.

RANDOM 1: Shit, man, what's her problem? She got into La Crosse.

RUPERT: Don't know, man. Want to do some dog?

RANDOM 1: Sure.

RUPERT (Internal thoughts): As I take out my wrap of dog, I look up at the sky—it is azure and calm. It's beautiful. There are blue tinges and a cloud that looks like a llama.

RANDOM 1: Hurry up with that dog, man. I've got Mandarin class.

<u>10:50 a.m - VANDERMARK—OFFICE</u>

I'm interviewing Horatio Thompson-Davies. He's not been attending school for the last two weeks. I'm very concerned as he should do well in the exams but what I'm hearing is not good for our statistics. He's launched into an impassioned tirade on the disadvantages of a good education in the ultra-modern age.

HORATIO: You know, you can sit here and bollock me and try to get me to be a better pupil but what's the point? Look at the reward for all my hard work—after seven years in this crap-dungeon—if I work hard enough—then I get to go to university, where I'll get into 75,000 pounds of debt, I get to eat beans on toast and not go to lectures and spend my days working crappy jobs so I can buy beans on toast, then I get a worthless piece of paper because I've tried to learn something meaningful like philosophy—then I'm no better than I was before—except I've wasted five years on pointlessness, which has cost me

75,000 pounds—so then I scramble to find a dead-end job so I can try to repay that money which takes me my whole life—then I get a wife, kids, car and have to work all the time so I can spend two weeks a year in Spain with these strangers known as my family—then I get old and have to keep working because the government and the banks have fucked everything up—and so I die working and I have no definite answer or confirmation that I am going anywhere better—so I ask you—what the hell's the point in any of that?! Why sign on for a life of boring crushing certainty?—There's no guarantees—so why do that when I can say to you right now—fuck off! Fuck your fucking A-levels! Fuck your predicted A-star grades! Fuck your university! Fuck your debt! Fuck your predictable projected career path! Fuck your cardboard cut-out family! Fuck your demise into working death! Fuck your uncertain afterlife! Fuck it all and stick it right up your tired stereotypical bullshit rectum! I'm outta this school, out of your predicted grades, out of your league tables, out of your success-story bullshit and definitely out of your office, fuck-head! Have a predictable life! (Gets up and starts walking out.)

VANDERMARK: What happened to you? You were a promising student. What brought all of this on?

HORATIO: I tried LSD three weeks ago—you should too.

Horatio slams the door and leaves.

VANDERMARK (Internal thoughts): He's right of course, not about the acid I mean, but it still doesn't change the fact that we've just lost another positive statistic. Shit the bed.

<u>10:51 a.m - SOMEONE SOMEWHERE</u>

I remember when I was eight and we were called into the office of our principal in junior school. We were all in big trouble because we had been caught wearing toy cars in the playground. We had started doing it because our favourite New Grime rappers were doing it at the time—and their videos were all about them being in school and they wore little plastic toy trucks, tractors, cars, and combine harvesters on little chains around their necks.

New Grime was big back then and we were really into it because they were just a bit older than us and we thought they were really cool. So we'd save our money and go into town to the vintage toy store, buy a toy tractor or car or combine harvester, and buy a little chain at the bargain store and wear it around our necks at school—we used to think we looked so cool.

But one day, one of the female teachers—Mrs. Rycheque—started shouting at us and called us perverted and we all ended up outside the principal's office. We were standing outside there not knowing what we had done—our parents were called and there was a massive fuss.

It turned out that in London, school kids had started to wear these plastic toys as sexual connotations—a car meant you had a girlfriend—a tractor meant that your girlfriend was a goer, a combine harvester meant you had a big cock, a truck meant you liked it raw without a condom.

After that there was an assembly and they were banned from school property. Of course, everyone immediately went out and bought them and wore them under their shirts—the local store completely sold out of combine harvesters. I've still got mine.

<u>10:52 a.m - MARTHA TRUEBERRY—ENGLISH CLASS</u>

I'm sitting in class taking sneaky bites from a massive bar of chocolate I've got hidden up my sleeve. My concentration's always better when chocolate's involved. When I do my volunteer work at the RSPCA I always munch on big blocks of chocolate when I'm on the phone to the people because it makes everything better. I like cats but I like chocolate better.

<u>10:55 a.m - RUPERT—ON HIS WAY BACK TO CLASS</u>

I check my iPalm to see that I have a message from my mother on Mugbook!? I don't know how she has managed to find me on Mugbook—my address and area are encrypted—this is troubling.

Anyway, she says that she has heard from Princeton today and, provided that my results are good enough, I can sit preliminary exams with them over the summer and go to their 'Interview, Engagement, and Plyometrics Camp' in August.

I should be happy, excited even, but I'm so tired of all this bullshit right now: the revising, the applying, the coursework, the interviewing, the endless droning struggle...Is it all worth it?! The only thing that gives me any pleasure anymore is dog—speaking of which, time for another bump methinks.

11:01 a.m - VANDERMARK—OFFICE

I'm continuing my rallying of the ailing pupils. In front of me is the Benidorm twins who've been flaky and could possibly be a no-show tomorrow. With any potential runners, we intervene to try to make sure they don't leave the school before their exams are completed.

VANDERMARK: Right, Malaga and Madrid, I've been reviewing your predicted grades and it's important that you revise for tomorrow—so I'm giving you the option of our overnight study camp. You'll get tuition all evening and early tomorrow morning—all food and drink will be supplied and you'll sleep in the drama studio—we've imported some very comfortable beds—and so you'll be fresh and ready to start your exams. This will really help you and give you every chance of scoring an A* in your exam—what do you say, girls?

BENIDORM TWINS: No.

VANDERMARK: Girls, I can't stress the importance of these exams—with good results you could go to the university of your choice.

MALAGA: Don't care.

MADRID: Going back to Spain after this anyway.

VANDERMARK: Is there nothing I can do to change your minds?

MALAGA: Can we go now? We've got happiness class.

The girls get up and leave; Vandermark looks furious.

VANDERMARK: Dumb scum.

11:15 a.m - MARSHALL BACKTHWAITE-ERNST (18)—LIBRARY

I'm in grade twelve and don't have exams until next year but I believe it is always important to be prepared. So I am revising and I'm quite tired so I'm yawning.

Then suddenly someone taps me on the shoulder—I turn to see a tall strange-looking guy with pale skin and dark curly hair underneath a tall black top hat.

He pats me on the head and says, 'You're bored, aren't you. Let me help you out then. Since boredom advances and boredom is the root of all evil, no wonder, then, that the world goes backward, that evil spreads. This can be traced back to the very beginning of the world. The gods were bored; therefore they created human beings…'

He stares into my face—his black eyes attempting to pierce mine—I'm uncomfortable so I look away.

He whispers into my right ear, 'You're welcome.'

11:30 a.m - RUPERT—HUMANITIES CLASS

I'm listening to Miss Troy drone on and on and on, and I'm bored, bored, bored, bored, bored. The spiral shapes that I've been designing on my iTop's Etchamood facility are testament to this—swirly shapes that just go round and round—over and over and over again.

I'm bored and I don't think it's just the tremendously tedious pep talk that Miss Troy is delivering that's boring me. I'm painfully aware that it's several minutes since I did my last hit of dog and I need another.

It's not that I'm addicted, but I made a deal with myself to keep taking dog until after the exams or at least until college and I don't like to let myself down.

I raise my hand, make an excuse that I need to go to the toilet—something about a urine infection or crabs or something—she is so caught up with the love of her own voice and the love of her droning boring notes that she doesn't even pay attention. She just continues on and I leave the room—walking past 'Pepsi' Michaels who is snoring by the desk at the door.

I walk down the humanities corridor—the smooth deep blue carpeting is supposed to put us at ease and there's no doubt that it feels good underfoot—the signs on the wall are all positivity-related—various quotes from different happiness-based philosophers—big smiling faces—the video walls play messages from various sponsors wishing us luck on our exams and reminding us that we still have enough time to put in our sponsorship applications for college—Subway, Pepsi, Coca-Cola, Applesoft.

I've seen all these webverts a million times. They're all there—big cheesy junior executives doing the opening spiel—then it cuts to young models talking to each other in fashionable bars and clubs—wearing fashionable clothes and all the people who don't have sponsored names are ugly and are portrayed as losers while the sponsored people are all shown winning at sports, succeeding in their exams, walking hand-in-hand, laughing, going out with each other—while the nonsponsored ones are alone in their rooms, crying and looking suicidal. I pass a year-ten or year-eleven student who is looking up in awe at the screens—almost dribbling when the screen reveals how many eurocredits you get for signing up.

He'll be contacting them soon no doubt—only problem is I can sense his disappointment when the sponsors, one after another, tell him, 'Sorry but we're already oversubscribed in your area,' meaning 'Sorry but you're not thin enough or attractive enough for us.'

I pat him on the shoulder and whisper in his ear, 'Don't believe the hype, chap—they're all wankers.' He looks confused and I leave him to ponder this thought as I progress up the corridor.

At the end, I turn the corner and head into the languages corridor—where the soft carpet of the humanities corridor turns to deep red. Everywhere there are old Chinese proverbs about the power of positive thinking and smiling Oriental faces. The China-India pact make them our allies now, I suppose, and if you learn Mandarin, there's always the chance of a glittering career in Asia ahead of you but it's bloody hard to learn Mandarin and most of us drop it by grade eleven.

My old Mandarin teacher, Mrs. Miu, walks past, big grin on her face, and says something in Mandarin. I say 'Whatever' and pass quickly. Mrs. Miu freaks me out—she never speaks English as it's her philosophy that we'll only learn Mandarin if we have to work out what she's saying—pretty harsh philosophy if you ask me—and probably a very key reason why 75 percent of us dropped it.

I look in on a Mandarin revision class where Steve Travis is looking bored and listless. I get his attention and gesture as to whether he wants to go for a line of dog but I'm quickly met with the angry glare of Mr. Lu—who starts making his way to the door—and not wishing to incur his notoriously harsh words, I move on with pace. I'm just turning the corridor into the 'well-being' department when I hear his rant echo down the corridor behind me.

The well-being department's walls have endless pictures of successful athletes, positivists, and slogans about healthy living: recipes, mantras, chants, etc...the well-being studio is alive with the sound and sweat of a jazzbike class—the reluctant pupils being blasted up and down big virtual hills on their jazzbikes for an hour—all part of the government's wonderful scheme to make a daily hour of exercise mandatory—unless you've got a medical complaint as that would negate the government's mantra of every pupil being entitled to a state of 'well-beingness.' Motion-posters with mantras of 'Will yourself to be well' shout out at the poor gym rats as they pedal away.

Many of us have forged medical slips or we got our parents to pay off doctors to get us out of the exercise or we injured ourselves on purpose, and some of us even got incapacitated along the way—developing illnesses and complications from overtraining.

These days, a lot of old contact sports like rugby are frowned on as they are deemed to be against the tenets of well-being—but non-contact football still goes on with the proviso of immediate red cards for players that make contact with one another.

I look in on the panged pained expressions of the jazzbike class. They're sweating profusely but the jazzbike's hydration system keeps them going—they're all looking ahead—trying to concentrate and then I realize what's going on. They're in a revision class. The well-being teacher at the front is leading them through a happiness revision class—he's jumping back and forth by the whiteboard—leading them through the key tenets of joy—the whiteboard showing pictures of happy people and happy habits.

Watching the torture of these poor unfortunates makes me feel better—but what would make me feel even better is some dog. So I unwrap myself from this little moment and move on.

Going round the corridor I almost walk smack into Chris O'Reilly and a couple of his Hatter cronies. I exchange a nod with Chris and then him and his gang go off up the corridor where I hear them shout insults at the jazzbike class. Meanwhile I see the toilets and my anticipation builds—dog will soon be in my system once again.

I push open the door to find the toilet empty—perfecto—I take out a sign from my bag saying 'out of order' and put it up outside the door.

I close it up, and using the keys I stole from the cleaner, I lock up the room and move over to the washbasin area. The interactive speaker system says, 'Hot or cold?' I say, 'Neither—off,' and I take out my wrap of dog—not much left. I've already hit it hard today and I'll need to secure another wrap after school.

I could go to see Chris but his stuff is weak as his cronies do too much of it and then have to sell it watered down in order to pay their supplier. The mystery is who their supplier is—nobody knows.

I've known Chris for years. We grew up together in infant school and beyond—we were good friends—even earlier on in high school we were tight—but times change and he certainly changed a lot when he got into the gang thing.

Still, I've never seen him more happy or confident than when he discovered a talent for beating people up, selling drugs, and spouting bizarre philosophy—he really found his niche.

I sprinkle what's left of the dog—a big fat line's worth—on the counter, chop it up, and funnel it down my left nostril (the least-blocked nostril)—relief, exhilaration, and happiness follow.

Concentration levels go back up, focus back up, determination back up—I'm ready for my humanities class. I take the empty wrap of dog and throw it in the recycle bin. 'Recycle,' I say. It crunches up the wrap—destroying any evidence. I unlock the door and am met by Mr. Adams staring at me.

MR. ADAMS: What are you doing in here? Don't you know this toilet is out of order?

RUPERT: Oh, sorry, Mr. Adams, I didn't see the sign—I had no idea, I was so desperate to go that I must have overlooked it.

MR. ADAMS: But the sign's clearly visible.

RUPERT: I've been so tired lately, revising all night you know, I'm half-asleep—just didn't see it.

MR. ADAMS: Okay, okay, take a Relaxio or something tonight—but only a half—make sure you have a good sleep—it's important that you're alert and ready for tomorrow. We don't want you too groggy though so remember to just take a half.

RUPERT: Absolutely, Mr. Adams.

I lose composure and concentration for a moment and try to stifle an involuntary sniffle. Adams senses something is awry.

MR. ADAMS: Errrrr? You weren't just doing dog in there were you?

RUPERT: Dog, sir? Me, sir? No, sir, I can't stand that stuff or the people who do it.

MR. ADAMS: Oh, good, okay—on your way then—you'll be late for humanities class.

RUPERT: Exactly, and I don't want to be late for humanities, sir.

MR. ADAMS: On your way, Mr. De Richenbach Hoffman.

As I leave, I see Mr. Adams lock the toilet door—the dog is really kicking in now and I feel primal.

11:40 a.m - MARTHA TRUEBERRY—TOILETS

I'm not going to my last lesson as I'm hungry and need to eat some chocolate from my chocolate box—I made sure to leave a big block of milk chocolate for this afternoon and I can't wait to sink my teeth into it because it's chocolate and I really like chocolate.

12:17 p.m - ANDERSON MARR—DINNER HALL

I am standing in line to go into the eating area. Someone with an absurdly large hat is ahead of me. The queuing light says we have another five minutes to wait. I use the time to check the stock reports on BloombergAM—the behatted individual turns to me and says:

'You know what Kierkegaard said—"At the bottom of enmity between strangers lies indifference." You would do well to remember that.'

I am too busy checking my stocks to pay this supposition proper attention but am amused by his little quote. He accosts me again:

'He also said, "A man who as a physical being is always turned toward the outside, thinking that his happiness lies outside him, finally turns inward and discovers that the source is within him."'

My stock in Haliburton has gone up a few points. Good, this makes me happy—as evidenced when I check my serotonin monitor, which has gone up several positions.

The queue time now says, 'Two minutes.'

A female brushes past me on my left-hand side—dressed in a military jacket and fluffy bubble dress. She looks a bit like Lindsay Lohan did in her younger days: attractive and feisty, fiery-looking, she seems angry, but seeing that she was the one who bumped into me, I consider that rude but no matter. 'Watch where you're going, asshole,' she shrieks at me.

I have no desire to engage in conflict—my levels are reading at too stable a level, so instead, I simply meet her stare head-on with a benign gaze of my own that I have formulated to evade conflict.

Her harsh stare changes (it is obvious that she is extremely angry, probably a militant judging by the way she is dressed, and looking to take out her anger on someone) to confusion—because I am not reciprocating the conflict, then to attraction (after all, I'm relatively good-looking and was even approached about modelling by some disagreeable friends of my mentors aka my parents).

I see her lose herself (for a moment) in my deep intense gaze—she is melting. Then she quickly corrects herself and alters her welcoming smile to savage fury as her behaviour protocols reconfigure themselves.

'Watch where you're going I said.'

And she is on her furious way—storming up the corridor to find a new reason to be angry.

Interesting: It is moments like these that test an individual—interaction, engagement, propensity, factors that cannot be foreseen or prepared for, only work-shopped and considered—but the bare fact of its happening without your choosing is not up to the individual...It's purely visceral.

Clearly I felt some affection for her and she too for me—but I have engagements, objectives, places to attend, and factors to achieve—I cannot digress off this path—and she too clearly has a mission, albeit briefly interrupted by a momentary option—a new alignment, if she was so willing to pursue it—an optional road of romance, love, and affection as opposed to the river of anger she consumes herself with.

But she made her choice and so did I—to follow our original protocols. I check my readings—yes, good, all is functioning normally, except my heart rate, which is obviously a bit higher—understandable with all things considered.

The queue sign has gone back to 'five minutes' again. No matter, I look through the revision notes on my iPalm and the behatted individual turns to me again:

'Did you know that: Because of its tremendous solemnity, death is the light in which great passions, both good and bad, become transparent, no longer limited by outward appearances.'

I nod complacently and go back to my iPalm. I can anticipate another piece of cod philosophy coming from captain hat-features but he is interrupted by the loud buzz-saw ring of his iPalm. He looks at it resolutely and barks into its interface:

'I've told you never to disturb me during the hour of luncheon.'

The change in his demeanour is palpable. His facial complexion has gone from a seemingly self-amused, self-assured smirk to a malevolent diabolic churlish grin—his facial muscles inflamed with anger (something must be catching)—or perhaps these people around me are not keeping their sodium levels in check—high sodium levels do cause an explosion in anger after all.

'Well, if he still hasn't given you the credits then beat the living shit out of him...No, fuck it, keep him there, I'll do it myself!'

The behatted man suddenly storms off up the corridor in fury. There must be something pervasively insidious about the design of the dining hall corridor: the beach brown yellow wallpaper that was designed to pacify the students is having the opposite effect. That's clearly what's causing all this angst and aggression.

Further up the corridor the hatman stops another student, a quite rotund one, much larger and taller than he is, and who, judging by his uniform, must be in grade eleven.

He holds him up by his shirt and shouts into his face:

'Listen, idiot! Did you know that Schopenhauer said: Life without pain has no meaning!?'

The hatman proceeds to punch the poor chap dead in the face.

'There, I've just given your life meaning!'

The year-eleven falls to the floor and doesn't get up. The queue time now says, 'Two minutes.'

12:25 p.m - MARTHA—DINNER HALL

Everyone tells me that I'm fat but there's nothing better than chocolate. Sometimes I melt chocolate in the microwave and rub it all over my face and my belly. Sometimes I fill up my belly button with melted chocolate and let it set. Then I dig it out and eat it later on. It's always good to have some stashed away so that when you wake up in the middle of the night there's always a tasty treat nearby.

12:27 p.m - WALTER TRAFFIC (19)—DINNER HALL

It is lunchtime and I'm at the school canteen. The food is horrific: truly dispiriting. There is a brown watery slop (vitamin soup allegedly) and a large slab of barely cooked bread with a thin strip of stringy protein-plus processed cheese on top.

Years ago, you could get food of some substance, health, and choice at the canteen—but not anymore—now the food is truly horrendous. The school budget was shot to bits and the first thing to suffer was the canteen.

I opt for the mineralie pizza and hand over my four eurocredits. I go to the vitamin bar and ladle a big spoon full of 'tomato + sauce' onto my pizza and sit in the corner. I bite into my 'healthy pizza' and immediately lose the will to live.

Sometimes, I wish I did dog—it would get me through days like this.

It's all because of the damn government—after they introduced M, the logic was that you could eat anything the rest of the day (including brown slop or shit pizzas as mere filler) because your nutritional needs were already taken care of—not that this is the case though!

A lot of people believe that it's a government conspiracy and that M is nothing but a placebo—but attempts at an independent enquiry have failed as the government keeps shutting it down.

12:28 p.m - CHRIS—TOILETS

In the toilets, Chris and his gang have a year-thirteen pupil, Michael Satchell-Davis, up against the wall.

CHRIS: Kierkegaard said, 'Be that self which one truly is.' So, what are you? Who are you?

MICHAEL: I'm Michael Satchell-Davis.

CHRIS: No, you're not, you're a dog addict! A liar, a cheat, and a thief, and you'll also be deceased unless you get us our credits…So what are you going to do to make this right?

MICHAEL: Please! Just give me one more gram. I'll find the euros. I'm seeing my uncle this weekend. He always lends me money when I need it.

CHRIS: Not acceptable.

Chris uses his umbrella to stab Michael in the stomach.

CHRIS: Where have you been, Michael?

MICHAEL: I went travelling with my parents for a month—we did New Asia. I'm sorry, Chris. There was nothing I could do. It was last-minute. There was no way I could get in contact with you.

CHRIS: 'People commonly travel the world over to see rivers and mountains, new stars, garish birds, freak fish, grotesque breeds of human; they fall into an animal stupor that gapes at existence and they think they have seen something.' Is that what happened to you? Did you see *something*?

MICHAEL: Errr, yeah, I saw a few things—I saw Australia…

CHRIS: Hold him.

The others grab him.

MICHAEL: Please, wait! Let me explain! Let me speak!

CHRIS: 'People demand freedom of speech as a compensation for the freedom of thought, which they seldom use.'

MICHAEL: What the hell are you going on about!?

CHRIS: Discipline him.

Several of Chris's boys punch Michael in the stomach.

MICHAEL: No! I'll get the credits.

CHRIS: No—you won't.

Chris cracks the umbrella's wooden handle over Michael's head.

MICHAEL: You're crazy, man! Please! I'll pay you!

CHRIS: Don't call me that—'Once you label me you negate me.' Stand him up.

MICHAEL: Please, please! No! I'll...I'll...

Chris puts his finger up to his mouth and makes a shhhhhh sound.

CHRIS: Face the facts of being what you are, Michael, for that is what changes what you are...Now, I wish I could trust you, I wish I could entrust you with more dog and then get my credits on Monday, but you and I both know this won't be the case. After all, 'Faith is the highest passion in a human being. Many in every generation may not come that far, but none comes further.'

MICHAEL (Struggling): This weekend—I'll get it, I'll—

Michael is cut off by a jab to the stomach.

CHRIS (In a soft menacing tone): Stop lying to me and start telling me what you've got on you that can start making this right?

MICHAEL (Reaches nervously into his pocket): Here, here, take my iPalm... and here, here's my American Teen Card.

CHRIS: Pin number?

MICHAEL: What?

Chris cracks him on the head with the umbrella.

CHRIS: Pin number?

MICHAEL: 5467 Obama.

Chris hands the card to Butchy who uses the iPalm to call somebody. Chris smiles and stares at Michael who looks mortified.

BUTCHY: Yes, hello, I'd like to order two hundred credits to be picked up at 4:00 p.m. this afternoon from your Felixstowe branch...My number is: 5467 Obama...My name? It's Michael Satchell-Davis...Voice check? Of course. (He puts the phone up to Michael's mouth—Chris grins and glares at him.)

MICHAEL: Obama.

Butchy takes the iPalm back, listens, and speaks into it.

BUTCHY: 4:00 p.m.? Perfect, thank you, yes, you have an excellent and prosperous day yourself.

Butchy clicks the phone off.

CHRIS: Good boy, Michael, this and the two hundred credits will do for now—boys, clear him up—and escort him to the bank. I have a luncheon date to attend to. But before I depart, just remember this, Michael: 'It seems essential, in relationships and all tasks, that we concentrate only on what is most significant and important.' Understand?

Michael nods his head.

CHRIS: Splendid, see you soon.

<u>12:33 p.m - ELTON LABEQUE (19)—DINNER HALL</u>

I am handing out leaflets to students—reminding them to get registered for the elections coming up.

I am the Youth Party representative for Felixstowe and unless we really make an effort to change this country, the Liberals or BNP will get in and ruin our futures once again.

Now that Michelle Cotton is an MP for the Future Party we have seen a huge increase in membership. She had to quit her chat show but that is no great loss, as any way that we can improve membership and gain power is a just way.

Cotton is a natural leader. Who would've thought she had such substance, but her TV interviews and the manifesto she laid out in *Now* magazine have really shown that she has the chops to tackle the toughest issues.

She is her own person and is not afraid to take up a controversial viewpoint. Sure, she's been accused of arch-feminism but anything is better than the fucking Libs or BNP.

I pass my last few leaflets out and look up to see MTV blasting out the latest New Militants video, 'Happy to Be Hung.' It's a clever pun on the government's new happiness legislation.

Their video sees several kids at school decide to commit suicide—all with smiles on their faces. I'm surprised it's getting played. No doubt the government's happiness champion will request it to be banned soon.

The video finishes and someone turns the channel to News.com where Darcus Howe Jr. is being interviewed over his Black Party's recent run-ins with the Real BNP. Fights between the two parties have been a regular occurrence of late and both sides have been accused of approving these organised melees.

The news finishes and goes on to the new McDonald's advert, which is trying to peddle their GM-cloned *Wow It's a 'Cow' Burger.* This is supposed to be a healthy option as the McDonald's scientists found the healthiest cow they could and cloned it endlessly to produce the leanest and 'healthiest' burger.

12:34 p.m - SHANA—DINNER HALL

I'm sitting having lunch when I get a call from my parents. I put the phone to my ear while I take tentative bites of the soya sushi they packed me.

MOTHER: Hi, sweetie! How's your day going? Is it super? I bet it is! Ours is going fantastic! Just great!

FATHER: It sure is, honey, we're having a great old time, you should've seen how much paperwork your mother finished today, she's a super super trooper!

MOTHER: Not as much of a super trooper as your fantastic father though—he's a bureaucratic baron—a prince of paper—he's drafted a new serotonin bill already! Can you believe it?! I ask you, can you believe it?! Like, seriously?! How good is this man! Magic man! Marvellous man! Super daddy! Aren't you proud of your delightful daddy, darling?

Shana has her head in her hands.

FATHER: We've been getting so much done and having so much fun that we've decided to stay in the capital overnight so we just wanted to wish you a super swell sweet day and that we'll see you tomorrow night.

MOTHER: Best of luck with your exam tomorrow, sweetie! Love you!

Shana breathes a sigh of relief.

12:35 p.m - VANDERMARK—OFFICE

I'm eating my lunch and looking over my journal from the last few weeks. The entries are not cheering me up:

'Children—they are scabrous little leeches—thieves of my soul, baying for blood—they want to possess and envelope me—leave me a balled-up-washed-out wreck on the floor.'

Another entry says:

'I used to think vampires aren't real but they do exist and I know it too well—they're called teenagers and they suck all the life, energy, soul, and light out of your life and leave you a burnt-out husk dead on the floor and then they stab you in the gut, kick you in the balls, and blast you into the stratosphere. They must all die! Die! Die! Die! They must all die before they kill me! Yes, they must die! They must die! Die! Die! Die!'

Oh dear...

12:45 p.m - CHRIS—DINNER HALL

The beatings I've inflicted this week have emboldened and heightened my emotions. I feel visceral, real, potent, masterful. I unpack my lunch of poached salmon, raw broccoli, durum wheat pasta with low-GI tomato sauce, and vitamin water.

As I consume this repast in the luncheon hall I survey my fellow lunch mates as they try to eat the unwholesome sludge that the canteen has cooked up while others have sensibly brought their own morsels.

Nutrition is important if you are going to run a successful campaign in life and it is not something I balk at.

I alternate between reading papers—*The Times* and *The Guardian*—and watching the news bulletins from the school council on the Flashboard.

There are reports about the new Arab-Asian bloc's dominance of New World economics and their continuing military threat.

On the Flashometer, messages include: a memo about the school leaver's dance; something about Stan Rusinsky's dog being missing (I think I used to have geography with him?); the principal wishes everyone good luck in their exams; a memo about the late study sessions available at the school tonight and a reminder that you can still book your overnight bed in the drama studio or gym; the student council has a meeting at 1:00 p.m.; Stan Rusinsky's dog is missing; the school's McMorrison-backed soccer team are through to the regional finals and remember to do all your shopping at McMorrison's; Subway and Timotei have two more name-sponsored places—if you want to change your name and pay your way through university, then please see Mr. Freiburg; a reminder that playing Ninsega this close to the exams is a brain hazard and will severely affect your chances of a good exam result; Bethany Travis-Farqhuar sends her best wishes to all students (a hot-shot businesswoman who used to go here); Rusinsky's dog again.

I look to my left to see the Benidorm twins sit down and start tentatively taking stabs at their green salads. They are wearing short pink Nobu dresses and tight Arb fixings—yum yum, I wonder what it would be like to bang twins? I must find out.

12:47 p.m - ANGELES—BARNEY'S RESTAURANT

So I'm in town for lunch—some yurimaki salads with green fruit tea with some of my girlfriends from Deben and the Well-Done Academy—and we're discussing our recent lab surgery.

Labioplasty has just come back into fashion after a few years of it being frowned on. Girls now want nice big juicy vaginas like Tiffany Young (the porno-game actress).

We've all had ours done recently, except for Charlotte, and we're trying to convince her to go for a Tiffany, but she wants to be all new and go for a Missy Cyrus—the new American Queen Teen, whose ultra-small labia surgery has been leaked on the SuperNet.

Tara, my outspoken Well-Done Academy friend, is stirring up trouble.

TARA: So are you finally gonna go for it and join the rest of us?

CHARLOTTE: Well, yeah, my parents said that if I sit all my exams, then they'll pay for the lab surgery. My dad knows someone in the city so I'll get a reduction.

TARA: Great. So what are you gonna go for? The Tiffany, right?

CHARLOTTE: I don't know. I'm thinking about the Missy. After seeing the Internet pictures I think it could be the one.

TARA: Like she didn't know about that leak. Her people obviously leaked those.

CHARLOTTE: Did you see her mum on the news? Fuck! Was she pissed off!

TARA: She should stick to singing—and let girls choose what they want to do with their bodies. I mean, my mom was proud of my operation. I mean, she even got her own done after she saw how good it looked! Her mom's just jealous, I bet you! No seriously, girl! You gotta go for the Tiffany!

CHARLOTTE: But the Missy just looks cuter—and she's so hot right now.

TARA: Yeah, but what you have to understand is the difference between a woman and girl! Missy is a girl—and she went for a girl's labioplasty—a reduction for goodness sake! It looks so small and unthreatening, like she's apologizing for having a pussy for fuck's sake! Whereas Tiffany Young—now she's more like it! She's a woman, and everyone knows that every man wants a nice plump pussy. I mean they spend enough money and time jacking off in those replica pussies of hers. Trust me, if you get a Tiffany model, you'll never lose your man.

CHARLOTTE: Yeah, but Tiffany's like so last year—I mean most of you had yours done last year, right? And Missy is like so this year—she's the new hot pink! Her getting it done is so brave. It's like a statement considering who her mom is. She's saying, 'Listen, I'm not afraid to make my own choices—to grow up—to be a woman—to stand on my own feet.' Plus, Tiffany's pussy just looks like so big, it just doesn't look right, whereas Missy's is cute.

TARA: So what are you saying? You think my pussy looks ugly?

CHARLOTTE: Well, I don't know—I mean, I haven't seen it. How would I know?

TARA: Well, you have seen it, because if you're talking about the Tiffany model, then that's what I got—that's what we all got. So what are you saying?

CHARLOTTE: I'm just saying that I want a Missy—not a Tiffany. I think it looks better.

TARA: Well, if that's what you want, then you're a stupid bitch.

CHARLOTTE: Oh, don't be so childish!

TARA: No, I'm serious, we've made a statement with the Tiffany. You running off with your young childish Missy model—that's just you saying you're too immature to be with us. But before you decide, just hear from the other girls. Angeles? What does your boyfriend think of yours?

ANGELES: Well, as you know, I don't believe in sex before marriage, but I let Michael take a look at it and he creamed right there and then.

CHARLOTTE: Gross.

TARA: You see! The boys really like it. You should really reconsider it, Charlotte. Don't make the mistake of your life.

CHARLOTTE: I don't know—I'll think about it.

ANGELES: So, girls, who's out tonight?

SARA: Not me—I'm humping tonight! You see, Charlotte, my boyfriend can't get enough of my Tiffany, he practically worships it.

CHARLOTTE: Whatev...I've got evening study class at the academy.

ANGELES: Lame-oso! What about you, Melissa?

MELISSA: Maybe—I don't know? I should really study for the exam tomorrow.

TARA: Why bother? They'll pass you whatever you end up getting. Come out and have some fun instead!

MELISSA: Where?

TARA: Like the Grosvenor and then the Box probably.

MELISSA: Aren't you getting bored of it all though?

TARA: Yup—but we'll only be doing it for a month or so more before we go off to uni, so we might as well make the most of it—right?

MELISSA: Did you girls hear there's a pillow party on tonight?

ANGELES: I know—how lame!

TARA: Children will be children. Still, I almost feel like showing up just to show off my Tiffany!

CHARLOTTE: Don't you ever stop going on about it?

TARA: No, and neither will you when you get it done!

ANGELES: Did you hear that Michelle Cotton got hers done?!

TARA: You see, if a politician can do it, it just goes to show you that it's perfectly acceptable—even hip.

ANGELES: She's just trying to win the pussy vote.

TARA: Well, she's got it from me—especially when you look at the other candidates—what a bunch of lameoids!

ANGELES: I really hope they do something this year—I don't think I can take another Tory government—they're just so, so—

TARA: Lame?

ANGELES: Exactly, lame. That's the word I was looking for.

MELISSA: Whatev. Time to get back to class, girls.

<u>1:00 p.m - RUPERT—STUDENT COUNCIL MEETING</u>

Most of the upper school council are present. Our council is sponsored by Applesoft and their corporation rep, Michael Douglas Matheson, is here to oversee the meeting and give a speech. It's not long before he reverts to typical company-man type:

'Well, this is it! The eve of the big one! Tomorrow you become men and women! Citizens of this great world! Tomorrow you start the exams that will see you start the next chapter of your lives and become the future leaders of this wonderful world! The company is very pleased with the way you have represented it throughout your time here at the school. You have been one of the most proactive and professional councils we have yet to see! Sales of Applesoft units among students at this school have tripled since you took the reins of this council! Therefore, to express our thanks, I'd like to give you each the gift of these Applesoft laptops and iPalms and a year's free SuperNet access. The company would also like to remind you that we still have some places left on our rotating intern programme this summer. So if you're interested, call me. Okay, that's it—good luck and best wishes from all the personnel at Applesoft.'

Michael Douglas Matheson leaves the room.

ERNEST GRUNMAN-TURNBULL: Thank fuck he's gone!

MELISSA: I can't stand that dickhead.

SUBWAY (Fawning over the iPalms and laptops): Yeah, but look what we got! All that pandering to Applesoft has finally paid off!

MELISSA: You would say that, wouldn't you, *Subway*?

SUBWAY: What's that supposed to mean?

MELISSA: Work it out, sandwich boy.

SUBWAY: Hey, some of us weren't born with a golden spoon up our asses like you. Some of us actually have to find ways to fund a very expensive education.

MELISSA: Why don't you chase after him and apply for one of those internships already?

SUBWAY: I already have.

MARKUS: Okay, guys! Okay! Calm down! This is our last meeting, so let's not end it in bitchery! Right, I think we're all here, except Pepsi and Tarquin who are in study lab. But where's Harrison?

MELISSA: Looney bin.

LIONEL: Yup, he took too many learning drugs. It did his head in and he had a nervous breakdown the other night. I heard he was running up and down Hamilton Road naked, claiming to have found 'The Seventh Way,' whatever that is. Didn't you hear?

MARKUS: Poor guy, we'll have to send him some chocolates. Do we still have those gift boxes from Cadbury?

SHEILA: A couple, but according to our contract with them, we still owe them three more mentions and some project work.

MARKUS: Okay, then send Harrison a box and we'll shout out Cadbury at the Leaver's Prom—and we'll have a sponsorship banner made up. That should please them.

SHEILA: Okay, good, because one of their suits will be in attendance.

MARKUS: Harrison?! Makes you think, doesn't it? What's his condition?

MELISSA: Heavily sedated.

RUPERT: It could happen to any of us. We all take the same learning drugs, right? Guess it's just a lottery if you're one of the unlucky ones.

MARKUS: No, I think you're mistaken, Rupert! None of us take learning drugs. They are inappropriate and detrimental to our health.

RUPERT: Whatever.

MARKUS: Okay, well, let's get this meeting finished quickly so we can all go for our revision sessions. I only have two other items left on the agenda: Leaver's Prom and the new council welcome. Is everything prepared and ready for the prom?

MELISSA: Yup—the hotel is booked, the VJ and band are booked, although why we want a live band I still don't know?

RUPERT: I think they're quaint. It's what they used to do back in the day—nostalgia is a sadly overlooked emotion in this modern age.

MARKUS: Sure, then all we need to do is agree on the new council. The principal has proposed all the following members, which, as we all know, means these are the new members. (Passes photos around.) If we want any type of a reference we must be in agreement... New council proposal accepted?

Rupert's eyes light up in disgust at the proposals.

RUPERT: Jeezuz! Cyril Baxter-Youngman? Abigail Pension-Forthright! Miles Rydell-Pertwee-Malvern? These are all brown-nosing sycophants! They've all got their putrid dirty tongues up Vandermark's dark turgid hole! Really? Is this the type of people we want inheriting the council?

MELISSA: Don't you remember how we all got here?

RUPERT: Yeah—but we were never as bad as this lot! He's not even trying to be subtle anymore—I can't sanction this.

MARKUS: You know the alternative.

SHEILA: You were just as bad as any of them. When you campaigned you were Vandermark's number-one bitch, Rupert! So don't try and pretend you weren't! Just because you're about to get out of here doesn't change what you were or what you did.

MARKUS: Are we all in agreement? These are the new council members, right?

ALL (Except Rupert): Aye.

MARKUS (To Rupert): All in agreement?

RUPERT (Looking sickened and disappointed): Yeah—aye, whatever...

MARKUS: Good, I'll go and tell Mr. Vandermark the good news.

Markus walks out of the room leaving Sheila, Melissa, and Subway behind.

RUPERT: Cyril Baxter-Youngman?! For fuck's sake?!

SUBWAY: So who's going to the pillow party tonight?

SHEILA: I'll be there. I've got to unwind somehow before the exams.

MELISSA: Count me out—you never know who you're fucking when the lights go out—call me old-fashioned but I like to know who I'm screwing.

SUBWAY: Well, I'm going—my Subway rep says I can accumulate bonuses by going to any parties. As long as I get photos posted up on Mugbook and videos of me enjoying myself and being popular while eating subs, I can earn up to two hundred extra credits a week.

MELISSA: Sell-out.

RUPERT: So what's it like to be a corporation whore, Daniel?

SUBWAY: Fuck off!

SHEILA: Seriously though? Isn't it a bit weird being called Subway? Don't you find that people often call you Daniel? What do your parents think about it?

SUBWAY: Yeah—it's not easy--my mum was upset but my dad said it was a wise business decision. It was hard at first but it gets easier and now even my parents are starting to call me Sub. My mum once called me Subbie—I didn't like that.

SHEILA: Even your own parents?

SUBWAY: Yeah, Subway makes us carry a tracking device around so they can monitor whether people are actually calling us by our sponsored names—if they don't then we lose sponsorship money.

RUPERT: Do you get free subs too?

SUBWAY: 'One sub a day keeps the doctor at bay,' is what my sponsor told me. So yeah, I guess.

SHEILA: Fucking sell-out.

SUBWAY: You've told me that already.

SHEILA: Fucking gay sell-out.

SUBWAY: Yeah, thanks, Sheila.

1:10 p.m - JONNY HUSH (19)—RILEY'S SNOOKER CLUB

The Snooker club is cagy, dodgy, a perverse den of unseemly seediness. The men at the bar eat peanuts vociferously. The alcoholic dwarf woman bartender shuffles nervously—she's still hideously hung-over and is pumped full of coffee to get her through her shift.

The backroom has all the charm of a cancerous cave rat: rotten, old, decaying, underpopulated—too unprofitable to warrant an upgrade.

This place will continue to decay and get distressed. There will be no reprieve from its end. It will get knocked down to put up houses in a few years' time.

The patrons drink cheap beer and play cheap games of snooker. They will later go home to their cheap wives in their cheap homes, smoke cheap tobacco, drink more cheap beer, and fall asleep in front of their expensive plasma screens.

A troglodyte of a man is eating a mouldy disintegrating ham sandwich and talking about the weather to a disinterested old woman on the slot machines who is feeding a silly terminal all her week's wages. She won't be content until it's absorbed everything.

It's a depressing scene to say the least—but it's peaceful and otherworldly and I like to come here to unwind during school sometimes—just sit here and drink a beer while I write my journal in the darkness—listening to the soporific clonk of the snooker balls.

Everything is cool until we see some of the Warthog gang stride in: they're wearing their red and black colours. They make an interesting threesome: one is tall and skinny, another is big and blocky and the other one is very short—like five foot with a deep scar down his face.

They look like they're on some sort of a mission—which makes me uneasy. We just concentrate on the old school slot machines and try not to make eye contact. This is one of their hangouts but they don't usually come here until the night.

They go up to some of the workers and make light conversation. Then they turn their attention to the rest of us. I see Rudy, Marko, and Sergeant leave. They sneak out by the exit. I don't blame them. The Warthogs have been known to beat up people just for the sake of it. I'm about to leave myself when several of them block the exit so I try to play it cool. Two more come up to me: 'You go to Deben, right?'

I nod.

He gets right up into my face. 'You know Chris O'Reilly?'

'I know who he is—but I don't know him.'

'Can you get a message to him?'

'Yes.'

'Right, well, send him this.'

He takes my iPalm and transfers a message onto it:

'O'Reilly—rumble at New Allenby Park—10:30 pm. tonight. See you there and the rest of your Hat twats—X from the Hogs.'

1:28 p.m - RUPERT—MAIN HALLWAY

Anderson Marr is walking in front of me, walking? Or should I say gliding, almost hovering off the ground. Anderson's a weird guy. I never see him talking to anyone. He doesn't seem to have any friends or connections in this school. The only people I ever see him talking to, and that's rarely, are the school's faculty.

He wears a smart black suit, is always in black, and yet he's not pally with any of the Visigoths? He's academically brilliant, and yet he doesn't belong to any of the scholar clubs? He's even good at sports but he's not in with any of the sports lot?

The dude's an enigma, that's for sure. I once tried to engage him in conversation. Well, I won't try that again—just small talk, nothing big, I can't even remember what it was about now. Something about how the food at the school was getting worse maybe? I remember his head turning slowly and subtly to look at me, as though it was on a rotator blade—and his face—a glacial haze of impervious glass, every inch of it calm and studied.

He just stared into my eyes with his deep black pupils and then moved them slowly around in his sockets, studying every aspect of my face—I've never felt so penetrated in all my life. I've never felt so violated by a stare.

Then he just smiled at me, subtly, nonthreateningly, almost angelically and glided off to my right—the dude's feet barely seem to even meet the ground. I tell you, that was one of the strangest interactions I've ever had—since then, I haven't really felt the need to speak to him again, don't really see the point.

1:30 p.m - MARTHA TRUEBERRY—TOILET

For my second lunch I'm going to eat chocolate from my chocolate box.

1:33 p.m - SOMEONE—FUTURE MEDIA ROOM

Roy is showing me reloads of a stand-up comedian from the north called Yorky Porky—he's a large rotund offensive-looking individual who sports a bizarre headscarf, bicycle shorts, and a bright pink jacket.

He starts off his show with an announcement: 'All southerners are soft wankers,' and then goes into one of his catchphrases, 'Eeeeee by gum! Somebody just bummed me mum!'

He gets the crowd to repeat this as they coil over in laughter—many of the audience members are wearing his t-shirts and are holding up banners of his mum being bummed.

At the back there's a large projection of his fat northern mum—bent over in pain and clutching her ass. Every five minutes he'll turn to it and say—'Eee by gum! Who in their right mind would bum me mum!?' Audience members chime in and say, 'I would!'

At one point, an actress playing his fat northern mum comes out and he ends up pretend-bumming her. The audience reels about in hysterics as he says, 'Eeee by gum! Looks like I just bummed me mum!'

1:34 p.m - DNA MATLOCK—MAIN HALLWAY

Three years ago, the seniors all decided, well, about ten of them, to go crabbing the night before school, catch a bunch of crabs, and then release them into the school. They hid them in their lockers, and then at 2:00 p.m they all came out of class, feigning sickness and went to their lockers, took the boxes of crabs, and released them at various points around the school, and it was one of the weirdest things I've ever seen, scores of crabs all around the school, scuttling down the corridors. It reminded me of what we're like, what we must look like to the faculty, just a bunch of crabs scrabbling down the corridor, looking weird and vulnerable but ready to strike out in anger with our metaphorical claws.

I remember John Summers kept picking them up and throwing them at the wall, and then I remember Vandermark came rounding the corner and accidentally stepped on this huge monster of a crab. I remember the crunching sound and the way it splattered on the floor as his huge size-thirteen feet completely obliterated and destroyed this poor crustacean. I remember the way Vandermark's face changed to a look of shock, to horror to complete sadness, almost as if he was completely destroyed. There was a glimmer of empathy as he seemed to sympathize with the crab and then I swear he almost cried—he almost surrendered himself to tears.

Susan Meyers was there and she said she saw it too; she swore that she saw tears streaming down his face. Others say that after he'd squashed it, he kept stamping on it again and again, in a rage of absolute fury, foaming at the mouth and licking his lips with delight. Some even say that he scooped up the crab and shoved it in his mouth, eating the gory contents with relish, but this is pure nonsense, and it clearly never happened. I was there, and I saw it, and I tell you...Vandermark was visibly upset.

1:35 p.m - RUPERT—CORRIDOR

I'm on my way out of class when I see Jeffrey—haven't seen him in ages, he looks somewhat forlorn.

RUPERT: Hey, Jeffrey! Whaddayou say?! Haven't seen you in time!

JEFFREY: I can't talk right now, man. I'm in the middle of an existential crisis.

RUPERT: But I thought you got over that?

JEFFREY: I did—but this is a new one.

RUPERT: Damn, Jeffrey, don't you ever not have an existential crisis going on.

JEFFREY: Rarely—I'm nearly always in-between one.

RUPERT: What, one just happens and then you move on to another?

JEFFREY: Exactly—I get tetchy, frustrated when I solve one and I have an immediate need to move on to a new one. It's just the way I'm built.

RUPERT: So what's the new one about?

JEFFREY: They're always the same.

RUPERT: But I thought you just said that it's a different one now.

JEFFREY: It is but it's still the same.

RUPERT: I'm confused.

JEFFREY: Now you're starting to understand how I feel.

RUPERT: But what is it essentially about?

JEFFREY: Essentially it's about the same thing as before, the same thing as always.

RUPERT: Which is?

JEFFREY: I don't really know.

RUPERT: Okay, Jeffrey, I'll see you later, man.

JEFFREY: It's about the pointlessness of life—about the utter futility of doing anything—I mean, what's the point—there is none.

RUPERT: What?

JEFFREY: Well, if I do X, Y, and Z, then X happens, right?

RUPERT: What?

JEFFREY: Well, if I go Superline and buy something, then it will get delivered to my house, right?

RUPERT: I should imagine.

JEFFREY: Well, why? What's the point in that?

RUPERT: Well, you want something and you get it.

JEFFREY: Yes but why? What is the point in that? Why bother? And that's just a small example—but it applies to everything. There is no point in doing anything because eventually we all die. So really, what is the point in doing anything if we all end up the same, dead.

RUPERT: Then why do anything at all?

JEFFREY: In the forlorn belief that one day I or science might be able to conquer death—achieve immortality.

RUPERT: Well, that's a reason for going on.

JEFFREY: Yes, but the thing that grabs me, the thing that really gets me in the end is—so what?! What's the point? Why should we live for so long? Even if we were to achieve immortality—what does it really matter? What's the damn point?!

RUPERT: Well, at least if you lived forever, you'd have enough time to work out what the point is?

JEFFREY: But what if you work out there is no point—then wouldn't that be the worst—having spent all that time trying to work out what the point is—only to find out that it is a complete waste of time—that the point is that there is no point! Wouldn't that be ultimately depressing?

RUPERT: Well, it would be a little worse than that I expect!

JEFFREY: So you see my dilemma?

RUPERT: Yeah, I suppose so.

1:39 p.m - NIBZY—TV LOUNGE

I'm surfing through all the digi-channels that I can hack into on the school's system. I find: *Celebrity Shit-Can*—where Z-list celebrities try to shit into a Pepsi can—it is sponsored by Coca-Cola. My friend tells me that you don't see everything but you see enough—Dean Gaffney (He's going back to *Westenders* soon) won the last series. It's available to reload at NutsackTV.uk.

There is also *Celebrity Shit Fit*—where Z-list celebrities are driven to the point of insanity. Amir Khan lost it and went too far when Chip Matthews, the comedian behind the show, kept blowing balloon animals in his face—Khan whacked him and detached his retina—you can still buy the DVD of it from dodgy dealers.

2:00 p.m - MARTHA—TOILET

(Scoffing noises punctuated by the occasional grunt as she consumes a weighty chocolate-based repast.)

2:05 p.m - SHANA—CHINESE STUDIES HALLWAY

I'm walking to my Chinese literary class when it happens—I'm walking round the corner of the corridor when that jumped-up little whorebag Angeles runs into me and makes me spill my mochazappo all over my clothes.

'Watch where you're going, bitch,' I say.

She immediately slaps me in the face—saying, 'Filth like you shouldn't be allowed to walk around these corridors.' I'm shocked to begin with but then I quickly gather myself and land a punch right on her forehead which causes her to stagger back. Now she runs at me and attacks me with flailing arms.

It's at this point that Mr. Vandermark, Rupert, and someone I don't know interrupt us and break us apart. Vandermark tells us he hasn't got time for this today and that he'll see us in his office at three p.m. I won't bother to show up. He'll never remember anyway.

Vandermark—what a tool—and Angeles—that bitch's days are numbered—nobody hits me and gets away with it—let alone a jumped-up little cunt like that! I can't believe that bitch walks around alive—I'm gonna fucking kill her!

2:05 p.m - ANGELES—CHINESE STUDIES HALLWAY

Shana Capri is a skank bitch fuckhead! I'm walking round the corner from my revision class when the whorebag runs into me—throws her coffee over me and starts attacking me!

I'm lucky that Rupert breaks us up!

Vandermark just watches on and says something inaudible and some other geek asks me if I'm all right. Shana still tries to attack me but Rupert holds her back. I've got no time to spend with someone so insignificant so I throw her the finger and walk on. One must maintain some form of decorum when surrounded by such ugliness—life will get that bitch back in the end.

2:05 p.m - RUPERT—CHINESE STUDIES HALLWAY

So I'm hanging out by the smart-lockers, trying to calm down from a massive line of dog and I'm talking to DNA about aliens and the Chinese and whether the Chinese probes have discovered alien life and whether the aliens are in fact working with the Chinese and that actually he thinks that maybe the Chinese are actually aliens and that we're in trouble because of that—when suddenly, Angeles and Shana start going at it—firing punches and kicks at each other—a full-blown catfight!

DNA and I try to break it up and it's brutal: they're all over each other—it's only when Vandermark shows up and screams horrifically about the school and exams or something that they stop—they're shouting at each other as they walk off in different directions.

It all calms down and DNA starts up again about the aliens. He reckons Mrs. Hu, the Chinese language teacher, is one and that he's seen her glowing and talking some strange language into a little glowing yellow box that she got from her pocket.

He said she saw him looking and he's worried, worried what she might do. I tell him everything will be fine and that maybe, even if they're aliens, that maybe they're good aliens. He says, 'When did you ever see a good representation of an alien?'

And I say, 'Exactly!'

So he says, 'Maybe in real life, if they exist. Maybe they're actually not all that bad, maybe they're here to help us.'

Mrs. Hu comes walking round the corner and suddenly DNA isn't there anymore.

2:05 p.m - VANDERMARK—CHINESE STUDIES HALLWAY

Shana Capri and Angeles were fighting again. If it wasn't for my quick action, there would've been a major incident. Instead, what could've been catastrophic remained a small indiscretion. I caught the girls slapping each other and promptly separated them. Then, after apologising for their actions, they went on their way.

I don't need this sort of behaviour around exam time and I have no time to contact their parents, so I made the girls promise that this won't happen again. They agreed to resolve their differences and I wished them luck on their exams.

2:05 p.m - DNA MATLOCK—CHINESE STUDIES HALLWAY

I was chatting with Rupert about the mutations in people that GM root vegetables are causing in the Far East Block when Shana Capri and Angeles start a bitch-fight in front of us. It's not often that one is privy to such an amazing feat of seeing two of the hottest girls in the school engaged in brazen combat so I wait for a minute before I break them up.

Rupert was in some sort of a daze, dog-induced, no doubt—he's doing way too much of that shit—and he kept looking at me intently and saying, 'The Chinese eh?'

Meanwhile, the girls were going crazy and I'm getting hit but I'm not complaining—as sandwiched between the two of them, I feel really quite lucky. When will I ever get the chance of this again?

I see Vandermark watching us from the corner of my eye—standing in the Chinese corridor by the videophone. When he sees me, he springs into action, screaming something unintelligible at the top of his lungs. Then Rupert seems to wake up out of his reverie and he helps break up the fracas. Finally, Vandermark intervenes and the girls run off, spouting obscenities at each other; Rupert goes back to babbling about the Chinese then sharply exits when Mrs. Hu comes round the corner and then Vandermark collars me and tells me he's expecting big things from me in the exams.

2:06 p.m - RUDY (19)—SCHOOL CARPARK

So we're at Deben to make sure Chris and his hat wankers got the message about the rumble tonight. We're able to go through the school gate because Marko's brother knows one of the security guards (who used to be a Warthog) so we just pretend that we go to school here.

The first thing I notice here is the tension and the fear. There's none of that at the Well-Done Academy. We're told so many times about how successful and great we are by our teachers that there's a constant air of false positivity—people too afraid to be negative.

But here you sense there's an urgency in the air—something desperate—like everything might not be all right.

Apparently, Deben has to get really good results (90 percent A** grades or they are finished). They'll have to get merged with us (again) or be turned into a private business academy. Some say Applesoft might be put in charge of them.

You can see the stress and anxiety, the pressure in all the pupils and staff, but I really like the girls here, man. That's one thing I really like about this place!

Chris isn't here but I see a guy I know from his crew. I roll up on him: 'You get the message about the rumble tonight, man?'

'Yup—we'll be there.'

'Good—you tell Chris that—'

I get a knock on the head and turn to see Chris standing there with an umbrella and a big grin on his face.

'Hello, boys, how lovely to see you!' he blurts out in his arrogant drawl.

Then he spouts some nonsense from some bullshit philosopher he's always quoting.

He tells us to say hi to Mike who he put in hospital and says he's looking forward to tonight. He says he's going to put us all in the ground. Then he tells us to go.

I want to smash his head in but Glen holds me back. Glen respects Chris, says he's good in a ruck. I just can't wait until tonight when I can smack his stupid grinning face right the fuck in.

2:07 p.m - SHANA

I remember when I was ten, and Angeles and I were best friends—we would be round each other's houses all the time, which wasn't hard as our parents were and probably still are best friends. We would talk about music and boys and surf the SuperNet, talking to our friends and slagging off girls we didn't like.

I can't remember when we became enemies? Maybe it was sometime after we went to high school. We were split up into different classes and she found some shit slut whores that she befriended and she changed—like I didn't know her—a total overnight change—I swear the colour of her eyes even changed.

Full points for reinvention but it was not the kind of reinvention I could countenance so that was the end of a once-pleasant relationship. A pity as she was a cool girl once. But you can't tell a skank not to be a skank.

2:08 p.m - ANGELES

Shana never forgave me when her boyfriend, Daniel, kissed me at the first high school disco. That was the end of our friendship. After that she went all weird, disturbed, and militant.

2:09 p.m - SHANA

Angeles used to go out with this guy, Daniel, a complete loser, sums her up really.

2:10 p.m - CHRIS—SCIENCE BLOCK

I'm in my physics revision class—I like science—there's a certain determinism to it that cannot be invented—it's the logic of it that I like. There's no room for interpretation, no room for the in-between—it's all there—all clear—written down, in stone—like I said: determined. It's that supreme logic that you cannot argue with—I like that sense of supreme logic.

DNA Matlock is the most able physician in the class—he's a genius at all the sciences in fact. He'll presumably get all A**s—he's in the small cadre of pupils who are supposed to be the ones who'll pull this school through.

I'm one of those too. We all had a nice little tea party with the principal where he politely reminded us of our responsibilities and told us how important it was that we dedicated all our time to revising and revisiting the curriculum. To totally understand how important it was that we fulfilled our responsibilities, he showed us a film of athletes winning and of great scholars and leaders of our time—this little showboating seemed to go on for hours and hours—several people seemed to fall asleep if I remember correctly.

People at the party included Shana, who left after two minutes; Anderson Marr who seemed very attentive the whole time; Rupert De Richenbach Hoffman, who asked a lot of questions—that's old Rupe—dedicated but full of questions—always enquiring, always intrigued. This was a few months back—before his dog addiction really started to kick in. I'm worried about him now—he's using every day—I can tell—there's a certain look to dog users—I should know—I'm one of them, but I'm fortunate—I can keep my addiction under control—I use only once or twice a day, and my stuff is pure, which makes the side effects a lot less worse.

But Rupe—he's fucking up—starting to get that slight purple tinge on his skin. A few more months and it'll be full blown and that'll be it—he won't be able to go back to normal life again—once you're tainted, that's it.

I tried to talk to him two weeks ago—he was in Ruby's Café and I saw him as I was about to walk down Bent Hill.

He was lost in his iTop—drinking a double espresso mocha—his favourite.

I thought about it for a moment—I didn't know whether to bother him or not—whether to intervene or not is a key decision. I would never want anybody to tell me that I was using too much—I think I would actually punch their face in if they did.

But something got the better of me and I decided to turn around and go through the door. I ordered a cup of mojo extreme from Fat Larry—Larry has run the place for as long as I remember now—the place should be called Fat Larry's really.

Rupe didn't really look too pleased to see me. He seemed very engrossed in his iTop, but then again he hasn't really been very agreeable to me since I started leading the Black Hatters.

Rupe's never liked violence—although he didn't seem to mind when I used to stop him from getting beaten up by the other kids in primary school.

CHRIS: Yo, Rupe, how's tricks?

RUPERT: Hi, Chris, I'm just fine—have a seat.

CHRIS: That's very nice of you. What are you looking at?

RUPERT: Just Mugbook updates.

CHRIS: Anything interesting?

RUPERT: DNA's just cracked another major physics puzzle in the National Championships.

CHRIS: My guess is he'll win that thing.

RUPERT: Yup, he's only two rounds away from the final. If he makes it there, he's got it made—a full scholarship at any uni he wants.

CHRIS: I heard DNA wants to study in China.

RUPERT: Yeah, he's got a thing about those Chinese.

CHRIS: He'd be better off stateside.

RUPERT: Some might say.

CHRIS: Anything else?

RUPERT: Shana's bitching at everybody again.

CHRIS: Uh huh.

RUPERT: And apparently there's a rumble planned between you and the Warthogs tomorrow night.

CHRIS: That may or may not be true.

RUPERT: So how's your coffee?

CHRIS: Just fine, Rupe—how's yours?

RUPERT: Fantastic.

CHRIS: Ummmm. So you still with?

RUPERT: No. You seeing anyone?

CHRIS: I see a lot of people. I just don't see them very often.

RUPERT: I thought you had something going with Melissa?

CHRIS: Merely rumours.

RUPERT: What you up to this weekend?

CHRIS: Stuff...Listen, Rupe, I've been wanting to talk to you about something.

RUPERT: Shoot.

CHRIS: It's the dog, Rupe—I think you're doing too much of it. Why don't you give it up, pal?

RUPERT: Pot calling the Black Hat, don't you think, Chris?

CHRIS: This isn't about me, it's about you, old friend. Me, I've got nothing to live for. You, you've got passion, you've got drive. That's something to cling onto, that's something you'll lose if you keep fucking around with dog.

RUPERT: Is that right?

CHRIS: It's no good, Rupe, it'll fuck you right up—you might be okay right now, but after a while it'll really start to hit you—you'll regret it eventually. You'll start doing more and more and more and eventually you won't be able to stop—I've seen it before.

RUPERT: Of course you have—you knock the stuff out. Listen, Chris, I appreciate the concern but you've got nothing to worry about. I hardly use the stuff at all.

CHRIS: You got any on you at the moment?

RUPERT: Yeah, a little.

CHRIS: Is there ever a time when you don't have any on you?

RUPERT: Sure.

CHRIS: I think you're lying—I know what goes on in this town and I know you're using way too much, Rupe. I'm just asking you, I know we're not close anymore but I'm asking you, please, give up the dog.

RUPERT: I'm giving up after the exams anyway.

CHRIS: That's what you think, but the longer you go on using, the harder it is to stop. Stop now or regret it later, dude.

RUPERT: I appreciate the concern, Chris, really I do, but I've gotta go now. I've got an appointment with my neurologist. I'll see you around, chap.

CHRIS: Who do you see, Rutherford?

RUPERT (nods): Yup.

CHRIS: She's good—give her my regards.

Rupert nods and leaves.

CHRIS (Internal thoughts): You can only really try and tell someone once—when you've tried once then that's it—repeating yourself is ineffectual.

It's like if you tell someone that you love them. Once is enough. You do it again and you're just demeaning what you've said—watering it down to mean nothing. People can either heed what you've said, take it on board and respond to it, or do nothing. Rupe is either too far gone or not prepared to listen—probably a bit of both, but there's nothing I can do about it. You make your own bed, right?

<u>2:27 p.m - JIM MAYHEW-LIU—(18)—4D ROOM</u>

I'm sitting in the 4D room and I've hacked into the OtherNet. I'm watching some weird alterno-commercial about something called the Real Man Syndicate Institute.

It starts off with people walking down the street and then they're all turning into sheep and they start making bleeting noises—then they're being rounded up by a sheepdog and driven into a pen. Then they're being sheared. Then a macho voiceover starts:

'Have you often wondered why you're a sheep? Do you want to stand out from the crowd? Do you get tired of bleeting and sounding like a sheep? Do you have what it takes to become complete? Do you have a yearning desire to be more than you can be? Well, if so, then you should sign up for the Real Man Institute—don't delay, sign up today, the Real Man Institute has a fully comprehensive two-year programme that will immerse you in the dynamics of manhood.

'You will learn the five principles of manhood: respect for the self, servitude to the self, praise for the self, understanding of the self, and most importantly, tolerance of the self. So if you think you have what it takes, then maybe you could become a true and unadulterated Real Man! Sign up today for an exclusive prepaid twenty-one days—tax-on-top, service charge applicable, unfree free trial. Because remember: once you go Real Man, you will know yourself. The Real Man Institute's course is a proven and surefire way to accelerate your potential in this world. Don't rely on us, look at what our ex-members had to say about the process...'

A man is shown looking fat and eating chocolate bars and crying at his desk at work and then his head turns into that of a sheep (a fat sheep) and he starts bleeting. Then he runs around the office being chased by a sheepdog. All his colleagues are shaking their head dismissively. Some guy says, 'I'm worried about Tim.'

Then another suited guy says, 'I know, too bad he's just a sheep.'

An attractive girl says, 'Tim would be *so* hot, if he wasn't such a fat sheep.'

Another says, 'What a dipshit loser!'

Tim is eating food out of a trash bin when he stumbles on a flyer for the Real Man Institute.

He looks at it quizzically and starts reading—his head turns and it looks as though he's discovered something.

A voiceover starts: 'I was just a dipshit overweight sheepish loser but then I discovered the Real Man Institute. After signing up, within twenty days, my life had completely changed. After forty days I was unrecognizable—I lost weight, I toned up, and I became a winner.'

As this voiceover goes on, this fat man changes to a completely different person who comes into the office in slow-motion: he's thin, toned, wearing shades and chatting obnoxiously to all around him—everyone in the office is in awe and adoration of him. All the girls from before are falling at his feet.

A fit girl says, 'Wow, look at Tim. He's so hot.'

Another says, 'I know! He's just incredible.'

A dude says, 'Tim's the man. He's just tip-top.'

Another guy says, 'I wish I could be like Tim. He's awesome.'

Another says, 'The dude's a legend. He's got the full package.'

Then it cuts to all the dudes standing behind Tim in front of the Real Man Institute building:

'Well, now you can be like Tim too! Join today to change your ways! Be all you can possibly selfly be! Dream today to find another way! The Real Man Institute is your answer for a healthier, wealthier new day.'

Tim says, 'Well, what are you waiting for? Get your Real Man membership right now!'

It ends with a final voiceover: 'The Real Man Institute is your ticket to a new and wonderful tomorrow.'

2:29 p.m - SOMEBODY IN CLASS SOMEWHERE

I'm sitting in my advanced Mandarin class and someone mentions Sam Rusinsky and his missing dog. Somebody pipes up and says, 'Rusinsky? I think I take algebra with him.'

Someone else says, 'Didn't he lose his cat last year?' and someone else says, 'Who in the hell is this Rusinsky character?'

2:30 p.m - SHANA

Last summer I spent the whole time down the beach. Everybody would be down the beach—in between the Cliff-Tops aka Spliff-Tops and the Ferry. There was a whole stretch for about fifty metres that we took over.

We drank vermouth and lemonade, ate barbecued emu and quinoa burgers, sunbathed, and sometimes we would swim. They used to put something in the sea that kept it clean for the first hundred metres or so.

I was happy that summer—my parents weren't being so weird, I was going out with Rupert, and we would see each other every day. At the weekends we would go away to one of our parent's holiday homes in Blakeney or Walberswick. We watched a lot of horror movies that summer—but all from the nineteen eighties and nineties—the Nightmare on Elm Streets*, the original* Halloweens, Friday the Thirteenth, Waxwork, April Fool's Day, *etc…*

We would drink his parents' Chablis and make new cocktails like schnapps, cherry juice, and tonic. For dinner we would buy fresh fish from the beach and eat Tongan salads. Sex was the best it's ever been that summer—every night I looked forward to waking up in Rupert's arms on his parents' four-poster bed—the hot sultry sun would shine in through the bay windows and wake us up and we would make love some more. We washed a lot of sheets that summer.

It was a summer where everything seemed like life would be all right, like life was finally making sense, like all the years of misery leading up to this time was just practice. Seventeen seemed to be the year where my real life—a good life—would start—so much for that.

2:31 p.m - CLARE ASHCROFT-DAVIS (19)—LIBRARY

I am sitting in the library finishing my dissertation on 'Torture Porn of the Noughties.' I've been watching the *Saw* films, all fifteen of them, to support my theory that the Neo-Real wave of snuff films from the last few years is a direct continuation of the Jigsaw movies from the early noughties.

I think that watching all fifteen of them in the space of a few days was a bad idea and that's not because they're particularly gory but because the ultra-caffeinated Plus-Plus Stay Alert tablets I took to keep me awake for three days straight are now causing me to see some crazy shit that I hope isn't real, like the yellow dwarf-cat (half midget, half cat) who is trying to sell me tickets to the Baz Bernard show at the Regal next week.

He's laughing at me and telling me that he's my mum, then cracking up in hysterics, and then juggling toilet seats and then removing his head and replacing it with a pick-axe.

I slap myself hard in the face several times and shake it off. I get back to finishing the last paragraph and I am almost finished when I notice that I have a new message from Mugbook. It's an invite to a pillow party. I got an STD (rare these days) at the last one so I decline the invite.

Ever since they found a cure for most sexually transmitted diseases, everyone is a lot more promiscuous—orgies are back in fashion—and even our parents are at it.

I guess in a world so messed up and lacking in real hope a lot of people are going back to their base instincts and getting what little pleasure they can out of the world right here and now. That's all except the Neo-Traditionalists who prescribe to an almost Christian-like ethos of no sex before marriage but there's always people who have to be different. So it's up to them I suppose.

The dwarf-midget-cat is back and this time he's dribbling and he's got a jackhammer and he says he's going to use it to crack my head in. He says that once he's got access to my head then everything will be over and that he will live in my larynx for now until the end of time. I decide that now would be a good time to leave and try and sleep. Maybe if I sleep I will shake off the midget and foil his dastardly plans to conquer my larynx.

2:33 p.m - MELVIN MARQUESS-DEROOKI (19)—LIBRARY

I'm revising for my happiness exam tomorrow. It's drafty and cold in here—purposefully so. The school knows that when it's hot we get drowsy. So to keep us alert, motivated, and awake they keep it very chilly in here.

But today is a bit over the top—it's practically Siberian in here. You can actually see peoples' breath.

Mr. Sanders gave me a series of practice happiness exam papers but we all know that this will probably be the very same papers or close to them. I'm scanning the papers and doing some of the questions but they are impossibly easy and I'm really wondering why I'm wasting my time.

They're in multiple-choice format and it would take an absolute idiot to get them wrong. Well here goes:

Exercise makes us…

- ☐ Happy
- ☐ Complacent
- ☐ Angry
- ☐ Sad

Team sports make us…

- ☐ Elated
- ☐ Sanguine
- ☐ Antisocial
- ☐ Armenian

Endorphins are…

- ☐ Good
- ☐ Rubbish
- ☐ An almost extinct breed of porcupine
- ☐ A small boutique café in Skegness

Protein is…

- ☐ A good basis to build muscle
- ☐ A poison that makes us vomit
- ☐ A republic in Arab-Asia
- ☐ An amusing joke toy horse

What is the best aerobic activity to maintain happiness…

- ☐ Jogging
- ☐ Thinking about stuff
- ☐ Burning yourself with an iron
- ☐ Asking your dad for a fiver

How many times should you exercise a week…

- ☐ Between four to seven times
- ☐ When you feel like it
- ☐ Every five years or so
- ☐ Never—it's silly

I circle D and C for every answer, pick up my stuff, drop the papers in the recycling bin, and walk out of the library. I've heard there's some great new downloads from Scum.tv from the *Twat Factor* series—I think I'll go and check those out.

Twat Factor is a pay-per-upload show. It tries to find the stupidest and twattiest people around and just lets them talk and be themselves, and every week the untwattiest ones are voted off until the last one is standing and he gets a multimedia contract for a year.

The great thing about *Twat Factor* and Scum.tv is once you've paid for an upload, you can reload it anytime you want. I want to see the episode where Derek from Port Talbot burns his knob off with an iron!

2:34p.m - ARCHIBALD BRACKEN-TUSHKLEIN-THOMAS (19)—LIBRARY

I walk into the library. On the door is a digi-poster saying, 'Stan Rusinsky is still looking for his dog.'

Inside, the wave of cold air hits me like a cloak of ice. The librarian on my right sits behind her module, encased in mounds of clothing and a large fake fur coat.

The library is busy. Many of the students are doing last-minute revision and are sourcing quotes to use in their exams. Years ago, books became a thing of the past, but when it was confirmed that reading e-books could damage your eyes, the old-fashioned print came back into fashion.

I go over to the modern happiness section and check out Christopher Biggins's classic coursebook, '*I Packed My Happy Sack and in It I Put…*'

Biggins's large rotund botoxed face is plastered all over the front cover, filling every bit of space. I wonder how happy he can truly be, being that overweight.

2:58 p.m - SHANA—DAY-DREAMING IN HER EXAM-PREPARATION CLASS

Three years ago I went on holiday with my parents to a resort in Turkey. The weather was dark.

Every day they'd ask me if I wanted to go with them in their car as they went to explore the sights—and every day I'd say no and I'd sit in my room and cry for an hour or two, then I'd go into the bathroom and cry and sit in the bath and make the water really hot and pretend to make slits in my arm.

Then I'd make a noose out of my dressing gown and pretend to hang myself—if I really had the courage to do it, I would, but I lacked even the ability to do that. So I'd cry because I lacked the conviction to be brave enough to take the correct route out.

So then I'd go into my parents' room and into their bathroom and I'd pretend to swallow all their pills—pretend to down the lot in one go—pretend to stomach them—then practice writhing in agony on the floor as the pills took their effect—I'd rehearse writing on a small notepad: 'I'm sorry—but I couldn't take it anymore—I'm sorry—I'm so so sorry—it's my fault—not yours.' Then I'd practice the moment of death and imagine what it would feel like.

I'd even try to swallow a few of the pills but couldn't bring myself to, wouldn't bring myself to do the whole lot—couldn't really bear the idea.

So again, I'd cry—then I'd go and look at my scrapbook of celebrities who'd committed suicide and I'd kiss the pictures—and then I'd make drinks for the ghosts of the suicide people from my scrapbook and talk to them and imagine that they were giving me advice on how I could do it—how I could finish myself.

Then my parents would come home full of joy and exaltation and they'd ask me how my day was and who the drinks were for—and I'd go into deception mode and tell them how great my day was—how I'd been out enjoying myself with the people I met the other day—how they were on holiday from England like us—and how there was a girl exactly my age and we'd talked for hours about books and how we'd made plans to visit each other in England—and my parents would be so happy and I'd catch one of them in privacy saying to the other, 'You see, there's nothing to worry about—I told you she'd be all right.'

Then they'd ask me if I wanted to go out to dinner with them and when I couldn't escape from it I'd have to go and I'd sit and chew my food without really eating it—and then when they were getting drunk on raki I'd wander off down back streets where I'd cry and scream silently.

I met a Turkish guy—late teens—who spoke good English—I let him fuck me—and then he drove me home on his motorcycle—he tried to come back the next day—he seemed really nice—but I couldn't handle the idea of having to summon up the energy to talk to him so I told him that I was a different girl and that the girl he'd slept with the other night was dead and that she was never alive and that he had no business sleeping with the dead—and that he shouldn't try to contact me again.

He said I was crazy and drove off on his bike—then I went back to pretending to hang myself—my mother caught me doing this once—she raised an eyebrow and said, 'Are you all right, dear?'

'I'm fine, thanks.' And she just shut the door and walked out. She never said anything about it again.

The rest of the holiday followed a similar pattern except the nights got more interesting as, just like my parents, I discovered a love for raki that helped eased my pain—and meant I had an alternative bad feeling in the morning, which distracted from my suicidal melancholy. Now I could blame my pain on alcohol poisoning.

When we got back from holiday, I had three successive (almost successful) suicide attempts—one by pills—but I was found unconscious and had my stomach pumped—I never tried that method again as it was too painful—then I slit my wrists in the bath—but again, my mother found me in time—in the last attempt I tried to run in front of a bus but it stopped just short of me.

Next time I'm going to try jumping in front of a train—I've been told that this is a fool-proof method—that what happens is that you don't always die instantly from being hit but instead you die from the sudden shock when you look at yourself and see what's happened to your mangled torn-apart body.

My parents have tried to send me to therapy, tried all sorts of things, but after every time it happens, I just smile at them and say, 'I'm fine now—it won't happen again.'

But I've realized that life is not worth living.

I'm going to try again tomorrow after my happiness exam—I like the irony of it. I've checked the train timetables, and if I rush from the exam, I can catch the Ipswich to Felixstowe train by the bridge down the street right after it.

2:59 p.m - DNA—AMERICAN POLITICS LESSON

So I'm sitting in my American politics lesson and the revision lesson is on 'Palingate' and we're being drilled on the 'Subway sandwich approach to essay writing.'

Subway has coughed up funds to help supply us with educational materials for the course and so we have to sit through 10 percent of the course being led by a Subway educational rep—who fills us with the sandwich chain's propaganda and tries to paint all other fast food as evil, and is now teaching us that writing a successful essay is much like making a delicious Subway sandwich.

The corporate hound continues his spiel, 'How you may ask? Well, it is quite simple—like an essay you need an introduction and a simple beginning, and so likewise with a delicious Subway sandwich, you need some delicious Subway sandwich bread—whether it be regular multigrain, Italian, Russian wheat, African spice, Suffolk cob, Nordic multigrain—that's your basis—that's what you need to pile on your ingredients—and delicious ingredients they are because then comes the main part of the sandwich and the main part of your essay and any number of delicious fillings from chicken parmesan to Turkish tuna, from Jimmy's Suffolk sausage to Nairobi goat—it's all there. And of course for the vegetarians there's Tenerife tofu and New Zealand herb-infused quorn among many others. Then just like in your essay where you need lots of quotes, references, and evidence to back up your arguments so in your sandwich you'll want lots of our delicious reproduced vegetables to add a healthy bite to your sub from tomatoes, onions, lettuce, and asparagus—they're all there to add to your sandwich to make it an overwhelming argument for a delicious tasty meal. Finally, you'll want to add a conclusion to your essay—and likewise with your sandwich you'll want something conclusive to make your sandwich that much more delicious and convincing—and that would come in the form of our tasty tangy sauce and spices range—from fiery Sumatran fire sauce to Italian olive salad cream to Turin tomato paste to sausage sauce. Subway has everything you need to make a snappy delicious amazing sandwich with a taste that's just out of this world and indeed out of the next world. And there you have it—the recipe for a great sandwich and a great essay—so look what I have here—the hotline to the nearest Subway outlet—so who wants to order one right now?'

The Subway rep has also spent endless time thrusting promotional packages in our faces—offering us lots of money if we agree to sell our names and become Subway name-holders. He often keeps us going right through lunch until he knows the canteen is shut and then he orders us Subway delivery at a 10 percent discount.

3:00 p.m - VANDERMARK—OFFICE

I'm sitting in my office finishing the paperwork for the performance management reviews.

I can feel my immune system breaking down. I am sniffling, my head aches. I'm shaky, depressed, and also more anxious than I can ever care to remember.

I take two lorazepams and two more M pills and wash them back with a mug of cold dark rum.

There is a phone call and I take it—Sidney Irving from the local press wants a few words from me about the exam farce. I tell him that he's got the wrong number.

He phones back again and I tell him that he's still got the wrong number. He insists that this is definitely the number.

I tell him that I've got things to do and I'm a very busy man and that I'd appreciate it if he didn't call me again. He asks me what my name is and I tell him it's MUSTAPHA GRAHAM PERCIVAL RIKITY ROBERT ALI BOBCAT KAMAL THE THIRD but that he can call me HONEY BITCH-TITS if he's my dad.

He asks me, 'What!?' and I tell him that I'm a dwarven bellows-mender who's gone type-two ape-shit, and I put the phone down.

I go back to my reports and inevitably the phone rings again:

'Herro! Isssh that Siiiiiidnneeeeyeyyyy!!!! Boyyyyyyyyyyy! How have youuuuu beeeeeeeeeeeeeeen!!?' I say in an accent I can only compare to a demented Irish-Chinese-Texan.

The response is determined and cool: 'I know that's you, Mr. Vandermark.'

'So sollly—yoooure veeerryyy missstaken—now—can I take your order pleasshhhh? We ave shrimp on speshial toray!'

'Mr. Vandermark, the exams begin tomorrow. Now it's widely believed that these exams are almost worthless, that with the year-on-year inflation of grades, and the teaching to the exam ethos that exists in all schools today, that the exams mean nothing anymore. After all, businesses and government employers now set their own exams for entry-level jobs and all universities require a series of their own tests and exams before they are able to offer a place. So surely these exams are worthless? What do you say to that, Mr. Vandermark?'

'Shorrryy, I didn't undershtand—did you say number twenty-seven and fifty-three? I alsho suggest the shrimp special—velly velly good.'

'Mr. Vandermark, what do you have to say about the worthlessness of modern-day exams? Please answer the question.'

I go into a heavy Texan accent: 'We alsho have spring rolls, prawn crackers, and ribs—will that order be for pickup or delivery, son?'

'Mr. Vandermark, I really need to know what you have to say about this matter? Please answer the question or I will be forced to print that you said examinations are worthless.'

Still in a heavy Texan accent: 'Now if I didn't know better, I'd say that you was a dumb, horse-shit-eating, pudwhackin' sonofabitch!' (In Chinese accent.) 'Now, will you be picking that order up or will it be delivery?'

'This is your final chance, Mr. Vandermark. Please make a valid comment.'

(In Indian accent.) 'Yess, sir! We have korma, madras, beef curry, prawn masala, and we have all your favourites here at the Raj Mahal Palace! Please be advised, sir, that we only take cash or eurocredit cards, you stupid bastard!'

'Very well, Mr. Vandermark, expect to read a transcript of this conversation in tomorrow's paper—I'll send you a copy.'

(In heavy Texan accent.) 'And I'll give you a good ol' punch in the fuckin' mouth, son! You stupid damn dipshit pudwhacker sonofabitch!'

The phone goes dead and I drink my mug of rum. I go to my filing cabinet, extract the hidden bottle of hooch, and replenish my cup. The lorazepam I took is starting to take hold and the dark oozy warmth of the luscious alcohol is washing out my insides—leaving me fuzzy and splendid.

Now the mountainous stack of paperwork doesn't seem so harsh. In fact, the rum addition has given me a better idea. So I take the stack of paperwork and start shredding it—throwing it up in the air—dancing around as I do so. It's confetti and I'm the bride!

I feel great. The combination of the rum and lorazepam has combined to make a championship team and I am the captain.

My iPalm rings—it is my wife. I switch the phone off and continue my office paper-shred dance. I add some music by turning on my iTop and I go to Radmusic.uk.

My dance intensifies and I'm twisting and turning and the stack of paperwork is disappearing. I'm so happy to be completing all this work in record time that when the stack has got down to halfway I reward myself with another cup of rum and another lorazepam—splendido!

Emboldened, the speed of paperwork is accentuated and before long I'm in a frenzy of paper-shredding, and when I'm not using the shredder I am tearing up the paper with my teeth and I'm throwing paper up in the air and karate chopping it.

Then I'm on the floor and I'm rolling around and tearing it with my bare hands. It feels great and truly visceral.

Now I'm exploding in hysterics of laughter as I munch down on Mrs. Dubrovsky's performance management review.

The paper tastes good, but it tastes better when watered down with more rum. I put my Cold War Kids on the iTop and start break-dancing.

I don't actually know how to break-dance but I do an approximation of what I imagine it to be like. I throw my arms about my head and do funky strange things with my legs. Then I put the webcam on.

I want to record these moments of breakthrough, this moment of transgressive freedom so that I don't forget this victory—this is the affirmation of a man's life. This is a hurrah for the spirit! This is a fuck-you to the moribund pressures of this comical and corrupt occupation!

Now I am bopping around the room—hopping back and forth. 'Hang Me Out to Dry' comes on and I'm twisting, turning, throwing paper up into the air, and knocking back shots of rum.

I need to urinate but I don't want to break this moment of excellence! I don't wish to leave this palace of fun! So instead of leaving my room I opt to piss in the bin by my desk.

The piss is excellent. It's long, languorous, and feels sweet to the touch. Golden reams of delicate dick juice decorate the empty and once worthless depths of a soulless paper-strewn wastebasket—bringing it alive with rich colour and wet delight.

The basket is just moments from being overfilled when I withdraw, holster up my penis, and continue my dance routine. The phone rings again so I wrench it out of its bastardly socket. Then evil emails appear on my iTop so I turn off the messaging system and kick the screen in until it smashes.

I take another lorazepam and drain another mug of rum and my routine reaches fever pitch! Excelsior! Huzzah! But what's that noise?! 'Tis several knocks on my door, which I ignore! Fortunately I've locked myself in my office so I'm quite safe and my fabulous new kingdom need not be disturbed.

I'm tearing up more paper and throwing it in the air so that it falls all around me like golden rain! My glorious parade continues! I can see the ticker tape! This is my chance! This is my moment! Oh my god, it's full of stars! This is great!

I'm twisting and turning—dancing like a ballerina, no, an Irish jig-master!

No! I'm the Lord of the Dance! I'm that Flatley fellow! This is fantastic! I'm in a fury of ecstasy! My arms and legs sending out messages of love and divinity to the crowd!

The people are craving me! Screaming for my attention! Happy to have me back safely! Well hello my people! It is I! I'm back! Have no fear! Daddy's here!' What more could they need! I'm here! I'm ready! This is it! This is it! This is it! Hallelujah! This is my time!!

The last thing I remember before I collapse is, 'Yes! This is what it's all about!'

Several hours later, I wake up on the floor with a wet warm sensation in my trouser groin region...I've pissed myself again.

3:05 p.m - RUPERT

My first proper date with Shana was when we went to see the new Saw *remake at the Champion's League SuperCinema. It was the first film to come out in 4D and everyone was excited. I was impressed and a little shocked that none of the gore and horror really shocked her, that she even seemed happy, impressed by it. But that sort of turned me on, I suppose.*

After the film we went for coffee at Ruby's and talked about music, books, and the future. I was impressed that Shana wanted to change the world. So many of my peers are just struggling to run their own lives, never mind thinking about helping others.

After coffee, I drove her back to her place on the cliff-tops.

She said she didn't want to go home yet, that her parents were still up and that she didn't want to see her parents, so we drove out to Gulpher Road and then down a deserted country lane.

It was cool down there—it was mid-December and the nights were dark and seductive. We talked some more about politics, about the economy, and then we made out. I remember thinking—shit! This girl really knows how to use her tongue.

She was a good kisser, deep, passionate, full-on, just like her views and the way she lived her life. Most guys like the girls who just sit there and take it, like dolls. What I liked about Shana was that she was alive, very much alive.

I had condoms with me, but she told me she would take a pill, so we made love in the back; after we finished, we shared a real cigarette, then it started to snow, light at first, then heavy. We stayed out there for hours, holding each other and watching the snow cascade down and cake the car, shutting out the outside world—you can't beat moments like that.

We made love again, then I drove her home. It was the best date I'd ever had.

3:10 p.m - SHANA—SOCIAL ROOM

I'm sitting in the social room, watching *A Clockwork Orange* on my A-pad—everyone else is on their phones or watching something on their devices as well—'Social Room'? What a joke!

I love this film, I can never get enough of it—it has a lot to say about modern society and the importance of the individual taking control—McDowell's character truly understands the importance of seizing control of your destiny, at all costs, even if it means surrendering your friends, family, and happiness—the truth, the true reality, this is what matters, none of the other inconsequential facets of life are important—only the truth, however horrible and horrific that may be—that is the only important part of life—only the brave and the resilient survive in this life. Conforming isn't surviving—that's just the surrender of your soul. Truth or nothing at all. Truth dammit!

3:12 p.m - RUPERT—TOILET

My dog days are becoming consequential. I just crapped out two huge solid purple lumps and my ass is burning, but I'll worry about that later. Right now I have to decide whether to do a massive line of dog or a small one. I end up doing a massive line.

3:14 p.m - MARTHA—LIBRARY

I've just been to see my chocolate box and the good news is I've had a properly good tuck-in and I'm now experiencing a post-box high. All the cocoa and chocolate is swirling around inside me and filling me with brown wonder, chocolate delight, and sugary love for the world.

It is at this time (before the big crash that will come in ten to fifteen minutes) where I am at my most sociable. In this small window of time I will make conversation, chat, natter, and flirt like I'm a regular person. Yes, I'll admit that most of this conversation is with myself or imaginary but at least I can have this dialogue.

Then, straight after that, as soon as the crash hits—I really don't want to know. I can be in mid-conversation and then I'll feel the crash coming—the sugar turning on me—all my elation dissolving into despair. I'll even start crying or I'll rush away. I wish that didn't happen.

3:45 p.m - SHANA—LIMOUSINE

I'm listening to my Earpod. It's a Sad Kate mix. She has the most fucked up but inspired lyrics like:

'Love is like a dead pigeon—it looks pretty and it smells of death.'

My parents call. I listen (painfully) to their very long message where they tell me (again) that they got so much work finished that they didn't need to stay in London after all and instead they've decided to celebrate with dinner in Felixstowe.

They tell me that they're going to help me prepare for my exams. They tell me that they are going to be my cheer squad. They tell me that after dinner we will revise and summarise and then say a 'Yes to Life' mantra before we meditate and prepare ourselves for bed.

I want to ring them and tell them to fuck off but relent when they tell me that they're going to give me two hundred credits.

4:00 p.m - RUPERT—BUS

I'm on the bus back from school and everything's pissing me off. It's that last day of school feeling and everybody's crazy. Some girl behind me has lost it and keeps gobbing off about a white ribbon until another girl two rows back comes up, smacks her in the mouth, and tells her to 'Shut the fuck up about the fucking white ribbon, you fucking twat!'

Then beat-boxing starts up with some of the rap posse busting out dodgy beats at the back. Then someone starts hiccupping and I see that Dwayne Thomas is demolishing a bottle of gin. He's gargling it noisily and swallowing it in great gulps.

It is offered to me but I wave it away. I just want it to be thirty minutes from now when I can be home and relaxed.

There seems a certain cruelty in having to sit in school all day after having been in a bus for half an hour, then having to sit in a bus all the way back for another thirty minutes. I look out the window at the graffiti on the sides of the abandoned houses. They're going to put up some more skyscraper apartment-style blocks apparently.

There's a bit of graffiti about Stan Rusinsky's dog and another bit of writing that says, 'Kill Everything Dead.'

The bus goes over a pothole and the bus shudders. This is great as it seems to shut everyone up for a moment but they are soon back to their usual bullshit.

I turn around and see the white ribbon girl is bleeding from her mouth. She's still babbling on but blood is coming out of her mouth now not words. The girl who smacked her is keeping a firm eye on her.

Behind her, DNA Matlock looks like he's working on a science project. I'm always amazed how he manages to get work done on this bus. He just seems to switch off and get on with things—he'll do well in this life. He's got a strange yellow pallor to him today though—looks very strange. He seems to sense me studying him; he looks up and meets my gaze, I smile to reassure him and he nods, then goes back to folding things.

There is a sudden boom as DwayneThomas shouts out, 'Rahhhhhhhhhhhhhh!!' He seems to have reached a gin-based crescendo of ecstasy as his eyes have a maddened delight about them and he's beating his chest in a pique of happiness.

The bus driver has finally had enough of the noise by this time. It's always the same. He'll ask in a polite voice for everybody to keep quiet for a bit then he'll shout, then he'll start screaming. Then finally, he'll blast the music up to its highest volume and sing along with the music—just trying to shut out the entire bus.

The songs are always the same: oldies from the 2010s *Best of X-Factor* and *Pop Idol* mixes. He reckons he was a contender in the regional rounds some years ago.

It's at this point that I wish I had a big gun.

4:01 p.m - DNA MATLOCK—BUS

I'm sitting on the bus and I'm trying to manipulate an experiment I've been given. It's a model and I must rearrange it to achieve optimum efficiency.

I am just about to reach a breakthrough when the Chinese alien woman materializes on the seat next to me—she turns her head slowly to look at me and puts her hand on my leg—she squeezes it gently and whispers, 'Soon,' into my ear.

Her breath is smooth and refreshing and tickles my ear. Nobody else seems to notice her as she continues to stroke my leg and whispers obtusely into my ear for the duration of the ride home.

4:05 p.m - MARSHALL—IN THE CHILL-OUT ROOM

I'm sitting in the chill-out room playing dominos. I got sent out for saying, 'All chicks have dicks.'

I don't know why I said it—it just came to me—it felt funny at the time so...

I'm looking on the computer to see what movies are on at the weekend: *Thai Stickman vs. The Beardy Weirdy* (a Thai martial arts/ horror/stoner comedy)—*When Two Are in Love* (romantic comedy)—*Dwarf Pirates vs. the Spanish Armada* (maritime period action thriller) that tells the supposedly true story about a group of small people who terrorized the Spanish fleet in the 1570s.

I hear it's fantastic. Several Hollywood stars signed up to be in it and had themselves digitally shrunken. One Hollywood star who starred in it said: 'It's not easy acting small, everything you do, you've got to do it smaller. You've got to imagine that you're three feet tall—you've got to talk lower. I spent a whole summer knee-walking in preparation for the role. I have a love scene with a real dwarf so I got some practice on that as well. You know, there's really not that much difference. Unless you've really experienced life as a dwarf, I don't think you can really play one. I also gained a lot of small friends in prep. I wanted to know what they ate, how they lived, what sort of jobs they do—it's a whole different world. But they're just like you or me, it's amazing.'

The other film showing is *I Never Agreed to That!* The synopsis says it's a screwball gross-out comedy about two husbands who turn gay and fall in love with each other—but are married to other women—so they all move in together and try an awkward foursome. Jack Black plays an overly amorous grandfather in it and it sounds shit.

4:15 p.m - RUPERT—HOME

I get home to find my brother passed out in the lounge. There's a bottle of vodka lying by his side. My brother's back from university in the states and he's not working. He's just been drinking (a lot) since he got back. My parents haven't said anything—despite the rapid way he's been depleting their liquor cabinet.

He wakes when I throw a cushion at his head. He manages a bleary-eyed 'S'happening, bro?' Then he falls back to sleep with a thunderous snore. I drop my stuff and head out into town.

4:30 p.m - DR. MACTAVISH—CLASSROOM

I'm marking philosophy papers on the metaphorical nature of depth and this is what Anderson Marr wrote:

'What is depth? That's a very good question. Depth is a full stop, depth is a comma, depth is logistical, depth is a strategy, depth is pragmatism, depth is contrary, depth is death, depth is sedentary, depth is unreliable, depth is optional, depth is something you obviously don't possess if you have to ask me such a weightless question.'

4:40 p.m - MARSHALL—WATCHING TV

I'm watching some dumb channel called Clunes TV. It just shows endless repeats of Martin Clunes–based shows—he's some faded celebrity from years ago. There's:

Clunes's Tunes—where Martin Clunes hosts a music show.

Around the World with Clunes in Reverse!—Clunes goes back around the world to the same places he has already been, to see if anything's changed (in the reverse order to which he visited them last year)—not much has changed.

Clunes Marooned!—Clunes is dropped off on a deserted island and left to starve and dehydrate while being filmed—at the last moment, just before he dies he is rescued and receives medical attention.

Cluedo with Clunes—a human-life version of the game with Clunes starring as Colonel Mustard.

Cluned—a TV sitcom about a future where Clunes is able to duplicate himself.

Clunes on Clooney—he interviews George Clooney

Clooney on Clunes—George Clooney interviews Martin Clunes.

Looney Clunes—where Clunes checks into an insane asylum and experiences life as a mentally ill man. He won a BAFTA for the latter and he thanked all the mentally ill people around the world for inspiring him in his speech. He said it was 'humbling.'

4:45 p.m - ANGELES—OUTSIDE THE NEUROPSYCHIATRIST'S OFFICE

I've just got out from seeing my neuropsychiatrist, Dr. Babcock. What a waste of time!

He asked me, 'What do the people who love you have to say about you?'

I said, 'The people who like me love me. They know that I'm gorgeous, generous, clever, ambitious, delightful, warm, enchanting, fashionable, diligent, open-minded, and liberal. They know that my best qualities are just being exceptional in every way. A lot of people are stale, static, and don't know what life's really about. But those who know me know that there is sunshine in my heart and they know that I can achieve anything I want. There are no limits to me. They know that I'm honest, progressive, and sensational. There's nothing I can't achieve. My best friends know that I want the best for myself and that there's a right way to do that. The best times of my life have been when I've achieved something spectacular.'

Dr. Babcock told me, 'Okay, Angeles, then what about the people who dislike you?'

'People who hate me think that I'm arrogant, self-obsessed, spiteful, sadistic, selfish, and a lot of words beginning with *s* actually! Have you ever noticed that? A lot of the words beginning with *s* are bad ones! Think about it: supercilious, sad, self-destructive. Anyway, back to what the idiots who don't like me think. They think I'm a tease when in fact I'm just hot and it's impossible not to be tempting to men by being hot! It's their problem, not mine! What else? Let's see. They also think I'm above them—which is probably true. Also, that I'm too good for them—which is also true.'

Dr. Babcock said, 'Who do you think is right?'

'Excuse me, is this some sort of a joke?! I thought you were supposed to be helping me.' Nobody knows anything!

4:46 p.m - DR. BABCOCK—OFFICE

I receive a lot of patient referrals from the local high schools. Mostly, they're from Deben. Shana is a particularly troubled young patient.

DR. BABCOCK: What was the worst thing that happened to you today?

SHANA: Coming here.

DR. BABCOCK: What was the worst thing that happened to you this week?

SHANA: Knowing I had to come here.

DR. BABCOCK: What was the worst thing that happened to you this month?

SHANA: Coming here.

DR. BABCOCK: I suppose there's not any point in asking you what the worst thing to happen to you this year is?

SHANA: No, there isn't.

5:00 p.m - RUPERT—RUBY'S CAFE

I'm sitting in Ruby's—drinking my third cup of coffee—and I've finished revising for my happiness exam so now I'm revising for my English exam.

This year we studied a module on alternative English fiction of the 1990s. We focused on the short stories of Will Self and *Tough, Tough Toys for Tough, Tough Boys* was our key text.

Apparently, students used to have to study William Shakespeare! Now, I know he's supposed to be a literary genius and a gem of the English lexicon but that doesn't make any sense. Why would young people need to study something so archaic? Thank god they found out he was a fraud—once that was established it was game over for ol' Shakey. At least Self's stories are relatively recent.

I shut my books—I need to take the sea air. I've drunk too much coffee though and I've been studying too hard all day—so I can't really concentrate. I go to the toilets where I dab some dog. It's good and strong so I do some more.

As I'm leaving the café, I swear I hear the young girl who's at the counter say to me:

'I've been watching you.'

I turn voraciously and corner her.

'What did you say?'

She's shaken. 'Errr, what?' She steps back.

I said, 'What did you say?'

'Honestly, I errr, I didn't say anything? Why are you looking at me like that?'

She looks genuine. She looks like she wouldn't say shit to a sheep to be honest, and then the strangest thing happens. Her head flips off her body and a little purple man with a ladder crawls out of her head, climbs to the top of the ladder, does a little back-flip, lands on the top of the ladder, and shouts at me with a Lancastrian accent:

'Marlowe! Merlot! Marlowe! Merlot!'

It's too much to take, so I leave abruptly, running out the door. I really must give up the drugs. But before I do that, I need a little line to steady my nerves.

Down on the beach I buy a Pepsi-vitamin from the Spa theatre shop and look at the acts coming up in the next few weeks: The Jim Davidson Five are playing, and no doubt their racist rock will bring in the local BNP crew; Pixie Lott (don't know who she is?); and Dick Jeffries the mad magician—I've heard of him. His act consists of turning himself into a rabid foaming lunatic.

The big piece he builds up to is when he cuts his knob off with a serrated knife. It looks quite real apparently.

I walk along the promenade and there's a lot of joggers, old people, and a few dog walkers. There's more of them when I walk along the Spa Gardens—quite ironic really—considering that there are a lot of dog dealers and addicts all along the Spa Gardens.

The Spa Gardens is a den of dog-dealing with spotters, holders, messengers—nobody who isn't dealing or buying goes in there anymore.

Then there are the bouncers who stand at all the entrances: string vests, huge muscles, Oakley's shades, baggy b-boy shorts, and sandals—all day and night they just stand there. It's a scene, man.

5:03 p.m - DNA MATLOCK—BEDROOM

Someone just sent me the New Militants' awesome new song—better than anything they've transmitted before. I like the Militants. I've been following them for a long time and I know a lot about them. They're connected to the New-Luddite movement, a rapidly spreading group of mostly young people who are committed to bringing the country back to the Dark Ages. Their motto is 'Absolute technology corrupts absolutely.'

Groups like PDC—Progress Destroys Civilization—are also down with them. They are well funded by rich anarchists, and activities include bringing down SuperNet cafés, wrecking 'equipment,' demolishing street infomercial displays, etc...They generally try to destroy things wherever they can, which is great.

Roderick Rage is their lead singer; their drummer is someone called Shit-Tax. Other members are Susan Strange, Mikey Madman, and 'The Shoe'—although 'The Shoe' isn't technically a proper member as he's simply a size-twelve black shoe that appears on all their tours propped up on a golden throne.

The members use The Shoe to beat themselves into a frenzy and this piece of footwear is accredited as having written all their lyrics and having produced all their songs. They maintain that The Shoe receives a fifth of all their profits. When asked once where The Shoe keeps his money, they nonchalantly replied, 'Where the fuck d'you think? The Shoebox.'

The Militants are from Milton Keynes. They are in their mid-twenties and have been going for at least a decade. They list their musical influences as: breadbaskets (the sound you make when you close them), Bach, The Sex Pistols,

Duran Duran, The Pied Piper, Sloe gin, Miss Charleton (their music teacher at school), and shoes of course.

A lot of their early work was about sex and relationships (this was before they matured and became more political). Song titles included: 'Put That Fucking Knife Down Before I Go Upside Your Head with My Erect Penis.' It's a touching love ditty about a boyfriend who is trying to calm down his jealous and mad girlfriend who's found out that he is cheating on her with her mother and furthermore he's bragged about it on Mugbook and posted up erotic pictures of her on social media.

It ends with them both killing each other and sharing a kiss before they expire. It was from their second album. The sparsity of its arrangement and the sharpness of its lyrics brought them a lot of attention.

'I Just Fucked Your Duck' is a coming-of-age story about the limits of trust. It tells an (apparently) true story about Mikey's upbringing on a farm in the West Country—a young man struggles to express his emotions and feelings to a girl he likes, so he symbolically reflects them by making love to one of her ducks. He films it and emails it to her. It ends on an optimistic note with the police unable to trace the sender's source and the boy moving on to having genuine feelings for the duck.

'Canned Cunt Blues' is a hard-rocking party anthem best taken with a healthy amount of Blodka. This is a raucous party anthem about a girl who drinks too much and crams strange canned goods into her love envelope. However, a can of mushrooms gets stuck up there for good and in coming years the girl is given to pine about her woes.

The band went through a stage of writing sex songs like 'Stuff the Muff,' while 'Head from the Dead' is about a happy-go-lucky poor sod who frequents graves to receive late-night fellatio from those who have departed this world. There's a funny bit in it about a worm crawling up his jacks-eye! It goes, 'Oh no! Oh my! Who would've thought that I'd die from a worm crawling up my jacks-eye!'

'Best Cock on the Block' is a straightforward bragging song. 'Ribtit Sunday,' 'Naughty Necrophiliac,' 'Sex and Slambuca,' 'Arse n All—and I Don't Mean the Team!' 'Pumping Pussy'—these were all songs they recorded in their sex phase.

Then there was the food album where they became obsessed with jams, cheese, chutney and the West Country.

They were going to a lot of village fayres at the time (having moved out to Devon to stay on Mikey's farm. This was a rare excursion into folk music and is best left forgotten.

After that they went through a dance phase where they took a lot of Ace (ACE)—acid and ecstasy mixed together—which many people, with a knowledge of drugs, consider one of the best and craziest highs ever imagined.

They would go to various mystic areas in Somerset: Stonehenge, Wookie Hole, Burnham-on-Sea, the Quantocks—and camp out for days under the influence of this stuff. Unfortunately, although it produced some of their most interesting music, it was also some of their most impenetrable as the arrangements were beyond abstract and the lyrics unintelligible as they insisted in creating a brand new language called Numganoo and singing almost entirely in this dialect.

With no way to decipher the lyrics (no translations or dictionary existed to decode the language) many fans were put off. This time took its toll on the band and all four ended up going to separate rehab facilities and it took a good year to sort them all out.

None of them will talk about this time and it is rumoured that they barely remember recording the album.

The *They March to Millbank* album was where the Militants actually started to embrace politics and began to turn into budding revolutionaries. This song was a call-to-arms to the post office workers who'd been disenfranchised and were left unemployed by the end of the traditional post office service (everything having been changed to electronic mail).

The government's 'Post to Coast' scheme tried to solve this problem by promising to get the unemployed post workers jobs in coastal resorts. This failed miserably when it was found out that posties were simply being offered part-time work selling ice cream and chips.

This taking-up of national and regional causes was a new direction for the New Militants. It was felt by some to be the time the group finally grew up and threw off their youthful directionless anarchism. This was further inspired by the lead singer attending Oxford for one year—only to be expelled for bringing an anteater (with a big sign emblazoned on it saying 'The Government') into one of the dining halls. Mikey later issued this press release: 'It's a statement about people being ants and the government eating them up like the cunts they are.'

5:05 p.m - CYNTHIA CARPATHIAN—BEDROOM

I roll over on my bed and my journal falls to the floor. I struggle to pick it up—but I have to—I don't want my parents to find it while I'm asleep. It's open on one of my journal entries—I read it:

'All my dreams are nightmares—all my nightmares are horrific. All my days are dark—all the dark is dead. In my bath I drown—in this life I frown. All the happiness is done—there is no more fun. Death is the only thing left. Of joy, in this life, I'm bereft. Fuck everything, life is shit, fuck everything—I'm in a pit. Kill the cows, make them die. Bugger the swans—until they can't fly. The ponds are filled with grit—the monkey's gone ape-shit. The golf range is gay and all the neighbours' heads are filled with hay. The trees are tall and of no use—for oxygen to prolong this miserable life, they produce. I will not go to the wedding—why should I? Why should I want to celebrate a pairing of people who are going away into their own miserable selfish existences. It's a form of death. The woodlands are fucked…'

There's another entry called 'Life' - Life is like a washing machine—it just goes on and on and on—turning around and around and around and then it ends. You start off dry, you get wet, and then you get dry. The only difference is that in the end with life you end up dirty and dead.'

5:07 p.m - MARTHA—KITCHEN AT HOME

I can't remember when first I tasted chocolate but I do remember that it was a special day. It was a day of rejoicing and merriment. I remember seeing it for the first time—the gleaming packaging—the wonderful words on the wrapper—the silky way it got undressed so delightfully. The soft brown textures melted tantalisingly in my mouth then slipped down my throat like water trickling down its favourite stream.

Chocolate was like an old friend that I hadn't seen in a while. Then I found out that there were different types of chocolate: caramel chocolate, white chocolate, toffee chocolate—a whole wonderful parade!

There were just so many different types and they were all my best friends! They are pals that I never get tired of and they never get tired of me. It's as though it's meant to be! This is it! This is the start of my life! And I've never looked back since.

My parents got my stomach stapled when I was twelve but I've since put the weight back on.

5:08 p.m - CHRIS—AFTER VISITING HIS NEUROLOGIST

I'm sententious (pompously moral) my neurologist says. He says that it's not a bad thing but he says it's something I need to get out of my system in order for me to be happy. He says I need to express this fully—develop a cathartic response to it. He told me to make a list of all the things I hate and dislike in the world. I don't know how this will help but I'm going to do it anyway:

1) Scofflaws—they need to die.
2) Idiots—no place for them in an educated world.
3) Myself—I could do better.
4) Zebras.
5) Presents—what's the point? They come from a false place.
6) Sports—a waste of energy.
7) Work—it makes you tired and depressed.
8) The sky.
9) The world.
10) Sleep—it wastes time.
11) Sheep.
12) Television—wasteful.
13) My neurologist.

5:25 p.m - RUPERT—SEAFRONT

I'm taking a walk along the seafront and trying to calm down from my episode in Ruby's. I'm staring out at the sea and realizing how beautiful it is.

After those two girls went missing last year, there were numerous sightings of them along the seafront—the weirdest ones were from people who were out in the early morning along the promenade—dog walkers, joggers, and revellers claimed that they'd seen two girls in the sea—bobbing up and down—waving their arms and singing out, 'Everything's all right, everything's okay,' over and over again in a monotone flat voice—and just as quickly as they were there, they were gone again—damn spooky if you ask me.

5:30 p.m - MARTHA—BEDROOM

If I had a superpower, my superpower would be to summon up chocolate whenever I wanted it. I would eat it all day and then eat some more. Then I'd kill everyone.

5:35 p.m - BARNEY 'KRISPY KREME' TUCKWORTH

I go for a walk in the grove to get sentimental. It's a wood at the back of the town. My analyst has said that I'm not in touch with my emotions and that I should do something to rekindle my feelings—he said to go somewhere where I was happy as a child. Well, I was happy here when I was a child—I used to enjoy walking my golden Labrador, Herman, for hours here. Herman was a stupid dog, but he was loyal—and he loved me to throw sticks for him, sticks that he would run after for a few seconds and then lose interest. We figured he had ADHD so we took him to the dog doctor who prescribed him Dogalino—a newly improved dog concentration enhancer. But it only seemed to make him more stupid: he would run after the stick and then just run off into the distance, and he would never settle at home, just roam around the house all day.

So then we figured that he had hyperactive issues, so the dog doctor prescribed him some sedatives but that just made him sleepy. He would just sit and sleep, he could hardly even be bothered to eat. The doctor said that the dog needed to engage with the medication for it to work, but when I asked him what that meant, he said that the dog needed to meet him halfway—when I asked what that meant, he said that usually in these cases the dog's owners were to blame and that, on top of the dog's medication, we needed to get some medication for ourselves so that we understood the dog. So we got some meds too, which made us hyper and then sleepy. When we stopped the meds (we couldn't afford them anymore), everything went back to normal and the dog just ran after sticks for a bit and then lost interest again, as usual.

But I enjoyed those walks, something about the trees and the trickling of the water and the leaves and the squirrels—and the way my dog would run after bits of sticks and then seem to completely forget what he was doing. Those were good days. I wish I could feel happy like that again. My doctor says I should go back on medication, and when I told him I was on too much already, he said that I needed to get some therapy to help me deal with my issues around me being concerned about doing too much medication. He said he could get me a special deal if I signed up today. I signed up, and now after school every day I spend an hour in the Special Centre listening to all the ways that my medication is good for me. Maybe it is, but then why do I feel like shit all the time?

5:37 p.m - ANGELES—HOME

I'm watching a really stupid show called *The Dude*. It's about this laid-back Californian guy who does really pointless things every week. Each episode has a silly title and premise and just follows him about while he really doesn't appear to do anything of any value at all.

This week's episode is called 'The Dude Wears a Snood.' He's just walking around his house and the mall in a snood and isn't even talking to anybody. It's just an hour of him mooching about in a silly piece of clothing, looking moody and not even interacting with anyone. Who watches this rubbish? It's even worse than last week's episode 'The Dude Is Rude,' which followed the dude on the beach as he surfs. Nothing happens for forty-five minutes—and he's not even a good surfer. Then at forty-six minutes in, another surfer almost cuts him up and he shouts at him, 'Hey, man! Fuck off!' And that's all that happens. The next fourteen minutes is just him walking back to his car with his surfboard, then going home and eating a sandwich.

There's twenty-six episodes of this!? I mean, really!? The week before that, the episode was called 'The Dude Is Pursued' and that was just the dude at the gym, then at a Subway, and then some girl calls him and says does he want to go to a party and he says no, and that's it. I heard that there was a time when reality television was actually relevant? Well, those days are long gone.

5:40 p.m - ANDERSON—STUDY ROOM

I'm writing a treatise on the nature of control:

Everything in life is control. The world will try to control you, therefore, it is imperative that you control it. Without control there is no forward movement. All your so-called friends, acquaintances, familial ties, peers, colleagues, etc...they will try to steer you in your life, try to bend your will to theirs, try to influence your thoughts, feelings, and systems. The only way around this is to control yourself. The only unfortunate part about controlling yourself is that you inevitably have to control others. But without this barrier, without the understanding of others' intentions, you are left vulnerable to their machinations, so it's important to launch a preemptive strike, to get around them, to absorb them, to subtly influence their concept of thinking so that you may maintain control of your own destiny. Without this attack, there is no control—you have to launch your attack, just as nation states influence others by diplomacy and physical attacks, but subtle diplomacy is always the desired option.

Fortunately, I have not had to revert to the acidity and horror of the physical attack, but it always has to be considered a possibility—a last resort to be countenanced should it become necessary.

5:45 p.m - VANDERMARK—OFFICE

I'm extremely concerned about the happiness exam tomorrow—and so I'm reviewing some of their midterm practice papers. They're not reassuring.

The question is 'What makes you happy? Explain in 500 words.'

MARTHA TRUEBERRY: Chocolate.

CHRIS: Doing the best for my family and my school. Civic responsibility is personal responsibility and that is the most important facet of a character's personality.

RUPERT: The asterisk key on my iTop.

ANGELES: Fashion.

SHANA: The thought of dead Tories' decaying corpses.

DNA MATLOCK: The idea that soon I won't have to answer stupid questions like this.

SUBWAY: Subway sandwiches—they're the best in the world.

Shit! This isn't good. I review the money section. It's key as we're supposed to instil in them the belief that money is the path to happiness. It doesn't look good either!

'What do you think about money?'

ANGELES: It's great and necessary—you can't buy good clothes without money.

SHANA: It's an instrument of capitalist Tory oppression.

RUPERT: It's okay.

ANDERSON: The bargaining chip of life.

CHRIS: It doesn't think about me and I don't think about it.

DNA: How much are we talking about? The Chinese will soon have all the money in this world.

SUBWAY: It's great—as you can use it to buy great value delicious sandwiches at Subway. There's a fantastic offer on from now until August 23. Eat superfresh and eat super free-range—eat Subway.

The next question is 'A place where you were happy.'

ANGELES: Milan.

CHRIS: The fourteenth century.

ANDERSON: This morning. I had a burst of excitement caused by a sudden rush of endorphins emanating from my workout.

SHANA: At the anti-Tory illegal rave last year in Rendlesham Forest.

SUBWAY: Subway. It's a great eating environment and a magnificent place to socialise in a stress-free location that is full of great people and wonderful superfresh and super free-range food. Studies have shown that people who eat at Subway are 83 percent more likely to be happy. Eat superfresh and eat super-free range if you want to be more happy—eat Subway.

The negative questions are also worrying as we train them to refute negativity. In the questions on 'miserable behaviour' they are supposed to put 'N/A' or 'I refute negative emotions' but sadly this has not transpired in their replies.

'A place where you were miserable.'

SHANA: Just about everywhere—this whole life is just one big capitalist lie—and you're part of it—so stop asking me these stupid fucking questions.

ANDERSON: Misery ruins your mood and affects productivity in a derisory way, so I try not to be affected by it.

ANGELES: The dressing rooms in London Hermes last week—nothing good would fit me.

CHRIS: There was a theme park I went to in a dream last Wednesday. There was a rollercoaster that was shut. That put me out a bit but it was okay because the Superkat Death Drop ride had just opened and I went on that seven times in a row.

SUBWAY: Taco Prince, Hunan House, McMorrison's, Delhi Hut, and all the other eateries except Subway. These places have been proven to increase your stress levels, leave you feeling depressed, and shorten your life, which transpires into intense unhappiness. If you want to feel happy, then eat at Subway, eat superfresh, eat super-free-range, eat at Subway!

'A place where you were angry.'

ANDERSON: Anger colours your judgement. It's something that must be manipulated and not indulged.

ANGELES: Paris.

CHRIS: Vienna, during the 1500s, fifteen minutes ago.

SHANA: My house, this school—every day, all day.

SUBWAY: Taco Prince, Hunan House, McMorrison's, Delhi Hut, and all the eateries except Subway. These places have been proven to increase your stress levels, leave you feeling depressed, and shorten your life, which transpires into intense anger. Studies have shown that people who eat at Subway eateries are 89 percent less angry than those who eat at other eateries. If you want to live a long life and feel happy and not angry, then eat at Subway—eat super-fresh, eat super free-range, eat Subway!

5:50 p.m - DNA MATLOCK—CINEMA

I pass by the cinema where they're showing all six of the *Shiteman* films, a series of cult films about a superhero who's composed entirely of faeces:

Shiteman 1
Shiteman 2—The Shit's on You
Shiteman 3: He's Free
Shiteman 4—Back for More
Shiteman 5—He's Alive
Shiteman 6—You're in for a Fix

Most of them are in 4D with the new Smellovision option. Barry Davis saw one and said it reminded him of when his badger ate some vindaloo curry and crapped it out all over his bed.

5:57 p.m - CYNTHIA CARPATHIAN—BEDROOM

I can't sleep—this much is clear and so I get up—it is excruciatingly hard and I almost fall over as I struggle to my feet. I have to hold on to the wall as I steady myself—I'll never get back to sleep unless I get up and walk about for a bit so that's what I'll have to do. To make it easier I take the amphetamine extract tablets that lay in the jar by the window and wash them down with a Coke Diet Extra—I shuffle slowly out of my room and walk down the corridor—everything in the house is dark—but I don't turn the lights on—I try to walk back and forth down the corridor but the strain is too much and I am tired—even though I know that I'm not tired enough to sleep, so I trudge into the lounge and slump on the sofa.

I just about have the energy to turn on the TV, where a rerun of the remake of *The Fresh Prince of Bel Air* is on. It's the episode where Philip Banks (played by

Lil Bow Wow) runs for mayor—and Will (played by Rudy Smith) takes the gifts of a girl he doesn't like.

I fumble in my dressing gown for my phone and turn it on. There are no messages except one from my phone supplier who tells me they have eighty-nine new deals for me to consider with a choice of 511 different tariffs.

I check Mugbook and see that people are going out tonight. I used to like going out—maybe if I take some more amphetamine extracts and drink a few more cokes I might have the energy to socialize. At least then I'd be out and I'd get tired enough so I could sleep properly.

I try to move but don't manage it until the third attempt—and I have to muster every ounce of willpower to make my way to the kitchen to get another coke.

The sun hits me from the windows as I enter the kitchen—the sun looks dark.

6:00 p.m - WARP HINDRANCE-THOMAS—TOWN

'Six o'clock: everywhere people are dead and they don't know it.'

They're moving into the nethersphere of the night. The sweet surrender to the day's oblivion—the nethersexuals are flocking in the courtyard—somewhere in some street, the gandyman is short-fisting the local cat. Across the street from him in a garage: a runner-up in life is gassing himself in his car—who will drink his vinegary homemade wine now?

Upstairs in his bedroom, his wife eats chocolates and sips mint tea—*Coronation Street* blaring in the background—no supper tonight, it's not important.

Down the avenue—at number forty-four, the old man hobbles into the kitchen and falls over, never to get up again.

At number sixty-five, the housewife calls her teen-toy-boy and tries phone sex for the first time.

Later, her husband will find out when the boy calls the house by mistake. They will divorce in three years—the husband considers it the best thing he's ever done. A year after that he will consider it the worst. Two years later, he gets over it when he finds love with an older man.

At the sports centre, the disabled action group are told that there is no more funding for their classes and that they are not welcome anymore. Most of them won't understand this and will need to be reminded for three weeks that this outlet is over.

A few days later, a community worker will take them for a kick-about with a football in the park. For her it's a great way to make herself feel better. She even keeps taking them out when she finds love in three months. She only stops the group when one of the 'specials,' Herman, gropes her breasts—'It changed everything,' she will say.

At number eighty-nine, Petrie Demarco makes a pizza and puts a slice of GM beef on it. He declares it a success and even sees fit to garnish it with oregano.

In the coffee shop, Isabel reads the local news on the company laptop and loses her job for wasting company time. Her indiscretion will go on her employment profile and she will find it difficult to get another job for eight months. In the end, her gay uncle will give her a job in his pornography business. Isabel will have great stories to share about gay porn at dinner parties for the rest of her life.

James is in the pet store having visions of genocide. All day he dreams about massacring all the animals in a grotesque orgy of destruction. He gets pleasurable sensations every time he thinks about what he did to the terrapins and he doesn't know how long he'll be able to control himself before he does it again.

At six o'clock, in four weeks' time, his mother will walk into the sea and not get out again. This will drive James over the edge.

'Six o'clock...'

6:02 p.m - ANDERSON MARR—HOME

I'm doing jumping jacks in front of the Bluescreen as I view today's world business report: Russian Standard has gained a majority shareholding in Nucleated Fission; New Zealand's economy continues to shrink by 1.2 percent a month—a worrying trend for the Kiwis who continue to migrate overseas at an extremely alarming rate; the American industrial arms complex continues to thrive as the chief sustainer of their economy—no surprises there; the people of Central Africa continue to be a force to reckon with now that they've put their differences aside and are united behind their great newfound mineral wealth.

Then it's on to the stock market and there's a lot of favourable activity in my sector that makes me elated. Later on I'll prepare myself a small organic salad and steam myself a side of omega-enhanced salmon, the perfect brain food for the mental journey of exams that I am to undertake.

6:10 p.m - ANGELES—HOME

I'm looking out of the French Sicilian fusion windows at the gentle swaying palm trees that line our street—watching the parakeets convalesce. Their bright colours blend in well with the lush colours of the trees.

I take a moment to yawn then return to the couch and continue to watch the fashion channel—which has a special on the forthcoming Durban extravaganza—all the top designers are going to be there and this panel show features some of today's big names.

They are trying to decide whether Durban has now eclipsed New York, Milan, Tokyo, and Dubai as the new fashion hotspot. They're saying this because there will be more designers than have appeared at any of the other shows this year.

I make a note to self to investigate airline tickets and routes to Durban. After all, I'm open to travel and I haven't fixed myself on London just yet.

I'm interrupted by a video message from my parents who say they want me to join them for dinner in town at the new Vietnamese place with Shana's parents. I respond, 'No, I'd rather die.'

They respond, 'It's good that you're concerned about your exams—there's lots of food in the fridge—good luck for tomorrow if we don't see you.'

I go back to the fashion channel where Chuck Hurricane (who is a transvestite dwarf supermodel from the Marshall Islands) is saying that we should be looking at the Durban Fashion Show in reverse and preferably through a broken telescope that has been smashed into pieces and taped back together awkwardly.

He says we should open up our minds to the prospect of something he calls 'Progressive-Regressive Durbania.'

When the presenter asks him or her (he has a sex change every season) what he means by this? He folds his arms, coughs, and shrugs, throws his hands up in the air, looks up to the sky, and shouts, 'Idiot!!' Then promptly waddles off set.

I'm interrupted by another message from Marco who says he's coming over. I try to message back to tell him not to but it is too late and he is already here.

He's at the door and our house manager, Shazz, has told me I have a guest. I could tell her to say I'm unavailable but I'd rather get this over and done with so I tell Shazz to make drinks and tell him I'll meet him in the cocktail room.

Several minutes later I turn off the fashion channel, put on my best breaking-up outfit, and walk to the cocktail room—only stopping for a short time in the mirror room to admire myself.

He's standing by the bay windows wearing shabby jeans, an ill-fitting shirt, and undesirable sneakers. The brilliant yellow sun is invading through the glass and shining on him in quite a romantic way.

He says we have to talk. I tell him that the talking is over and so is he. I tell him that after today he is not to come to the house anymore, call me anymore, or even look at me anymore. He is so destroyed it's almost pitiful. He has to sit down.

He puts his glass by the side and starts crying. He tries to talk but he is so choked up with tears that the words won't come out. I tell him to purge. I tell him that expressing emotion is good but that he only has a few more minutes to do it in front of me because then I'm leaving as I have to go out.

He keeps trying to say something—but it's just tears and sobs and cries.

The amusement of this wears off on me so I say goodbye and tell him that Shazz will show him out. I remind him not to call me ever again.

As I walk out of the door I can hear him garble something unintelligible through a burst of blubbering tears. I find Shazz and tell her to show him out and that if he does not leave, then Roderick, our security officer, should escort him to his car and not hesitate to use his zap stick if any trouble is given.

I go back to my dressing room where I prepare for tonight's pre-exam festivities: drinks at the Grosvenor and then on to the Horror Box I should imagine—hardly inspirational, but then again, a night in London or Ipswich is unfeasible tonight as one must be fresh for the morning.

6:14 p.m - CHRIS—HOME

I'm in deep thought as I stare at a framed picture of Søren Kierkegaard. I sometimes consult him when I'm at a crossroads in my life.

His responses are not always helpful but he can, on occasion, be quite insightful and useful, so I ask him, 'So are you for real or are you full of shit? Did you really believe in what you said or did you just profit from the vapidity and will to believe of others? Was there really any substance to your nonsense?'

There is a long pause as I lock eyes with him. 'I think you meant it didn't you? You dirty old dog, you actually meant and believed everything you said. Oh well, no matter, whether you meant it or not is not important—I don't care if it was all bullshit, because I know, I know the truth of everything...and that's a pretty heavy load to carry isn't it, Søren? That's a seriously heavy load to carry—you don't have to tell me—I get it...Did it comfort you, knowing that? Or did it just make your life worse? I bet it didn't help, did it? I bet it just complicated everything—I imagine it was what did you in, in the end. I won't make that mistake. I'm going to make sure I don't succumb to that horror...The abyss won't get me...It will try its hardest, I'm more than aware of that, but it won't win, it can't win. What do you say to that, Søren? Any thoughts?'

6:15 p.m - RUPERT—PROMENADE

I walk down the hill from the café and take in the sea air as it whips up at me. It's refreshing. The salt is tangy on the tongue and the wind and water are rejuvenating.

The joys of nature combined with the dog and the soy coffee is helping me to be reborn on this fine serene evening. The summer makes this town truly come alive and change in a most profound way.

Down on the promenade are lots of old people abusing fish and chips. There are always old people in this town. It's not for nothing that it's known as a retirement town—always has been, always will.

Then there are the dog walkers, the joggers, the couples, and the kids from school: getting high, smoking E-ettes, and wasting time.

Out on the end of one of the breakwaters, perched precariously, is Tim Mallard-Erickson. I'm concerned, no, maybe not concerned, but certainly intrigued, so I walk over to find out what's going on. He's holding his hands up to the sky.

RUPERT: What you doing, man?

TIM: I'm weighing up God and the Devil, dude.

RUPERT: What?

TIM: Good and bad—God and the Devil—trying to work out who's going to win. Trying to work out who I should follow.

RUPERT: Why?

TIM: Because you've got to follow something, man—if you don't, then how do you know you're making the right choices?

RUPERT: You don't think about it, dude—you just do it.

TIM: No, man, you've got to have a point of view, you've got to have a side. Now they've both got advantages so it's hard to decide—they've both got great power so it's tricky. It's difficult to decide, man. It's...It's difficult, man.

RUPERT: But surely you just keep going on—just keep going on and don't worry about it.

It takes Tim a while to answer as he keeps alternately raising one arm up into the air and then the other.

TIM: Negative. I've left it open for too long. I've been playing both sides, been a tourist in both camps, I've taken liberties—told God and the Devil to both give me a chance, that I just needed time to decide, but they've told me that's not fair. They've been sending me signals, letting me know it's not on, that I've got to choose between the two, that I can't have the patronage of both. I'm nineteen—no longer a child. I have to decide, and I have to decide tonight...They're not gonna wait any longer, man—unless I make a choice tonight, I'm fucked, they'll both desert me, then where will I be?

RUPERT: So you're just gonna stay out here until it comes to you?

TIM: Yup.

RUPERT: Well, good luck, Tim, I hope it all works out for you, man. I hope you make the right choice.

TIM: So do I, man. So do I...

I leave Tim to his soulful torment and go across the street to Gordy's where I order a rum and coke (ironically served to me by a girl called Coca-Cola—who's a hot-looking, Egyptian, Coca-Cola–sponsored exchange student). I sit and ponder good and evil...

<u>6:30 p.m - DNA MATLOCK—BEDROOM</u>

I'm sitting at my computer, trying to focus on revision when a flash-up message pops onto my screen in bright yellow. It's in Chinese and it says: 'Harken, for the day will be upon you soon—be ready.' It's only there for a moment and then it's gone—damn it, I've got to stop taking these learning drugs. Then the face of the Chinese alien woman flashes up on the screen and she's wearing a demented grin. She nods and winks at me. I quickly close the computer and rush to the bathroom to wash my face with water.

6:45 p.m - ARNOLD—MEGAMARKET

I'm at the Megamarket picking up some beer for the party tonight—I hate the megamarket.

These places are such vapid soulless horrendous places of disgust—I want to throw up in them most of the time. I feel like doing it right now. I feel like calling the manager over. The manager would come over to ask me what the problem was? He'd ask me what he can do for me. And I, very rapidly, would motion for him to come closer and I'd unleash a torrent of vomit into his face.

A real pretty river of patchwork sick that would cascade into his face, eyes, teeth, nose, ears—covering his whole head. Then I would shout into his ear, 'That's what's wrong! Your fucking store is wrong! It's a fucking nightmare of consumerist horror! It's wrong! Soul-destroying! Every single little fucking bit of it!'

Then I'd punch him in the stomach and knee him in the balls.

Instead, I stroll along the aisles looking at all the bullshit merchandise, merchandise they choose to rearrange every few months or so for no good reason whatsoever, other than because somebody has a job that involves strategic placing of food and merchandise to maximise sales.

I find the beer section and take down a six-pack of St. Peter's Punch (7 percent beer)—this stuff gets me good and fucked up and it's local so it wins on both counts.

I also pick up a bottle of Cheerio Whiskey—nasty cheap shit—but worth it for the sheer alcoholic buzz it will give me when I need it.

I saunter up to the checkout girl. I recognise her—she used to go to the school, years ago. I used to fancy her in fact—but she looks a lot older now—her looks battered and busted by the sick realities of her world. If she's working in here, then she's like all the other failures—couldn't get into a British university or college—let alone an American one. Now she's condemned to working here—that droned look on her face—like she's a total zombie—an automaton—only capable of picking up groceries—putting them through the scanner and into a bag. Well done, love.

I try to embrace her in inane conversation but she's lost—lost to the world for good—just another megamarket drone. Well, at least she has a life here—however mundane.

Her boss is probably even proud of saving her—reclaiming her from the failed clutches of a failed education system. How depressing...Man, I've gotta get drunk.

6:50 p.m - MARSHALL—BAR 130

I'm looking online at Club.com. I might go out this weekend so I'm looking at my best options in Ipswich and Colchester. This site has the best listings. I see that VJ Fucksticks is playing *progressive Witch House* at Club Cuntral. In the Bent Bender Room of the same club, they're having the *'I can't believe it's fucking Tuesday the thirty-seventh of July and I haven't been to bed for two years night'* Bet heads will be doing the new *Sheep Shake* dance there. It's a new look-move where you imagine you're vigorously buggering a sheep. Then there's the *Electric Turkey dance* where you imagine you're a turkey being electrocuted and you jerk around accordingly. You need a lot of drugs in you to do that one. The sick thing is that the VJ actually plays 4D videos of turkeys being electrocuted and sheep being slaughtered over the tunes. You can smell the blood and feel the fear of the poor animals as you jive and shake—a bit sick if you ask me.

Slambuca is the 'now' drink on these evenings, a very alcoholic drink that's a combination of Sambuca and Blodka (bourbon-vodka mix)—absolutely mental!

The dance I most object to though is the *'Arse yourself up the wrong un'*—it's a little jig where everyone tries to imagine that they're fisting themselves silly. It just looks dumb and is hard on the hips.

7:00 p.m - VANDERMARK—HOME DINING ROOM

I'm tucking into a steak and washing it down with an eminently quaffable bottle of Malbec. I drink at least a bottle of red wine every night—it washes away my nerves and makes everything nice and hazy and pretty and perfect. Two bottles is even better as stress completely dissipates and anxiety takes a vacation. Three bottles and it's all happy sailing into the midnight purple skies. Red wine is simply an educator's best friend. It's a magnificent pal of epic proportions. I once composed a poem esteeming my red friend's virtues:

'Thick red delicious blood of the grape—dripping down my thorax—coursing through my veins—filling and fulfilling my brain—making the normal seem strange and rearranging the mundane—building up beautiful enzymes and domains—harnessing everything within range.'

I've become a dedicated wine poet. Under any other circumstances, I do not do well with writing but when under the influence of the mystical red, I become a regular Rimbaud. I'm digging out my wine journal to reread some of my epic musings:

'Coffee!? Tea!? No, maybe wine?! Yes, definitely I'll have the fucking wine!—I'll eat and devour the entire vine! Give me grapes—give me distillation! I will form a brand new wine nation! We will drink from noon to three—canst thou not see how much pleasure I shall render to thee! Ha! Ha! Bacchus has offered me a charter! Let's get this party started! Faster! Let's go red! Let's go white! Tell you what!? You're both right! Rose can come if he wants too—but that soft little girly punk has a lot of front! To think he can be a part of this party!? But I'm generous so he can stay! Let's drink Rioja! Let's cane Pinot! Oh fuck yeah—I like my vino! You, me, Shiraz, and Merlot—we'll invent a brand new hero! Captain Cabernet is here to stay! Perhaps he'll lead us most excellently astray! Oh! The taste on my lips is sweet to the touch! Thank you! Thank you, Bacchus for this feeling so much! Oh wine! How I adore thee! For you have made my life complete—you make me want to traverse my feet! I'm in love it's true! For the freaky wonderful things you do! Thou art wonderful! Thou art divine! Let us build a brand new wine-soaked mind! Let's go mental! Let's go holistic! Let's go crazy fucking ballistic! Vino at the ready—wine on one! It's time to have some fucking fun! Word to Wolverhampton, wine is great—give me wine on an endless never-ending plate! I'll see you in the fields of joy—I've got a brand-new wine-based toy! Sauvignon Blanc is a pal for sure—perhaps you may require him some more? I shall let you partake—make no mistake—for this wine elixir is for everyone—a place of fantastic fun! Joy! Joy! Wine is here! Put away that gaseous treacherous beer! Not for me the bloating and cramp—I want something that leaves an indelible stamp—something that enhances the senses—sharpens the wits—something that leaves you in a fit—leaves you summoned and ready for more—ready to take you down to the core—makes you realize why heaven sings a happy song—so come now people! Don't prolong! Harken! Harken, I cry! Harken, I see Burgundy approaching! Yes, I vote as I be emoting! I want its silky goodness inside—let us now hasten and run to the tide! Let the sea of wine rush over you—splashing its goodness into your soul—this wine is blessed with a divine goal! It will cleanse your head and make thy furrow free! Yes indeed it is he! Mr. Burgundy has come to town—time for all the clowns to frown—for Mr. B is serious and true—for your liver he wants to renew! To leave it stained with his mark—to run up and catch you in the dark! All those wine stained nights return and to Bacchus's company you will return. For you are done on this mortal planet—now up to vineland you will ascend—it's time for you to start the real journey…'

Not bad if I do say so myself. Right now these precious grapes make a lot more sense than anything else in the world.

Only trouble is, one of our star-students, Harrison, is locked up in the nuthouse and we need him to sit his exam and do well so we can balance our stats.

For one reason or another, we've lost a lot of our students to the nuthouse in the last few years. Some say it's down to the pressure of the exams, some say the learning drugs are causing it and some say it's dog-related abuse. I don't know and I don't really care at this point! I just know that we need him to sit his fucking exams and get the fucking A** grades he's predicted or we're fucked!

The nuthouse is reluctant to let him out, so this is going to be a tough call. I think another few glasses of claret will relax me and temper my mood so that I'm able to converse pleasantly and let Dr. Renault understand our concerns for Harrison's mental health and why it would be in his best interest if he sat the exam.

7:01 p.m - DR. RENAULT—ST. CLEMENT'S HOSPITAL

I am going in to assess Harrison's condition.

At first glance he seems fine. He is sitting on a chair by the windows, looking out at the evening sunshine. He holds up his drawing for my inspection—it shows a man in a top hat being cut in half by a giant can of beans.

HARRISON: Yuckataaaaaabbbbyyyy!!

Harrison suddenly begins to jump about—imitating what I can only imagine to be a gorilla. Realizing that he is in no fit shape to sit his exam I make the phone call to his school...

DR. RENAULT: I don't think you understand, Mr. Vandermark, Harrison is not well. He's drawing pictures of people being killed by tinned beans and he's imitating primates. He's incapable of normal conduct...Mr. Vandermark!? There's no need for such offensive language! Mr. Vandermark? Mr. Vandermark?'

After such a brusque and threatening phone-call, certain procedures need to be upheld, so I make a call to security.

7:02 p.m - VANDERMARK—HOME

Fucking doctors! Think they know everything! I'll get that lunatic Harrison out of there by any means necessary. If he can hold a pen, then he can still sit that fucking exam.

7:20 p.m - RUPERT—BENOCHIO'S RESTAURANT

I hate this place—it has the discomforting feeling of golden pretension and a horrendously inept service to boot.

Someone, all of them, the staff, need to receive a good kicking for their lacklustre service and patronising smiles.

The tables are the colour of supercilious blue, and inconceivable imitation Mark Rothko murals hang on the walls. The cutlery is tin-latex—a new strange trend, and the tiling is hideous.

The skinny little hussy serving us is skinny, too skinny, but I'd still like to fuck her from behind, see what it's like.

I've never done that, never really fucked a really skinny girl from behind, wonder what's it's like? Must be interesting, I must make a resolution to pursue this.

The starters arrive but I excuse myself from the table and go upstairs. The one saving grace of this place is that they have good bathrooms to do dog in—that's the saving grace of most nightclubs and restaurants—without that, there's no point.

It's dark when you go in—then the lights, in the form of stars and planets on the ceiling, turn on when you come in. The fine yellow, lime-green china porcelain surface by the sink is perfect—long and clean enough to comfortably chop my dog up into two nice lines. They are quickly shovelled up by my eager nostrils as music by Stereolab plays on the in-room radio.

Suddenly, the colours change in the room and disco lights blaze out—but then I realize that this is only the momentary effect of taking too much dog! The high comes down and my euphoria kicks in—my hunger conversely dissipates—don't know how I'll be able to consume the very expensive food I've ordered—and I am suddenly as horny as hell! And I seriously consider leaving the restaurant and go straight to the pillow party but I know the shit that I'll encounter from my parents later on will be horrific so I return downstairs and ready myself for Act II…

The oyster risotto is actually not that hard to eat—and I don't know if there's any truth in the idea that oysters are an aphrodisiac or just that I'm feeling extremely horny, but my overwhelming urge to bend over the skinny waitress and deliver my rocket into her silo is reaching a critical level. A cheeky E-ette in the back courtyard smooths out my lust and I check my messages to see that the pillow orgy is definitely on.

Fuck it, I've had enough of this bullshit, so I mumble something unintelligible to my parents and rush out toward the exit—leaving my Galapagos lizard steak to go cold.

My father shouts after me, 'Where do you think you're going, young man?' I reply back, 'Yes, I know, I agree…'

As I leave I see the skinny fuck-candidate by the coat check and I tell her, 'I'm gonna have you someday soon.' I linger just long enough to see her shocked reaction change to a smirk, then bemusement, then a smile, and then shock again as I rush out the door—flicking my tongue at her suggestively.

The air outside is warm and enchanted with the rewarding fruit of summer exaltations. It is a fitting overcoat for my fuzzy demeanour. 'More dog!' I say to myself as I march stridently toward the party.

7:25 p.m - DNA MATLOCK—BEDROOM

I'm watching this new show on Scum.tv called *Pickle Dick, Onion Tits, and the Nob Juggler*. It's pretty shit. I really want to watch *Dat Crazy Sonofabitch* but my rerun rights license is expired. The China channel is showing *The Mandarin* so I figure I'll watch that for a bit.

7:30 p.m - SHANA—VENEZIA RESTAURANT

I arrive at the restaurant to find my parents sitting at a large table toward the back. They look happy—as always—but not forced happy (which is usually the case). Either they've done a lot of pills or they really have had a successful day.

FATHER: Darling! How wonderful! You arrived on time! How are you!? You look great!

MOTHER: Yes, darling! You look great! And I am very impressed that you arrived on time. Your timekeeping skills are really coming on, aren't they!

SHANA: Whatever. Did you order yet?

MOTHER: No dear, we're waiting for Angeles and her parents to arrive.

SHANA: What the fuck are they doing coming here? I thought it was just going to be us? Angeles better not be coming too!

FATHER: Language, darling! Let's not use such street-level profanity in a fine dining establishment like this.

MOTHER: Yes, please try to relax, darling. We wanted to celebrate our victory with like-minded people and you know how well we get on with them.

SHANA: Is that bitch coming or not?

MOTHER: If by 'bitch,' you're referring to Angeles, then yes, I believe she is, but please let's not have a scene, darling, just try to be amicable.

SHANA: If her dad brings up the Young Tories and tries to talk me into joining them again, then I'm out the fucking door.

FATHER: Well, you could do worse than join the cause, darling—the Young Tories are a fine organisation and your spirit, drive, intelligence, and energy would be a worthy asset to their cause.

SHANA: Do you want me to stay or not?

MOTHER: You know, we really did some great work today!

SHANA: So you keep saying.

FATHER: Ed's going to be very happy with our presentation—he's already received the first report and he's ecstatic.

SHANA: Ed Balls is an old freak and a fat wanker.

MOTHER: I'll pretend I didn't hear that.

The waiter comes over.

FATHER: Not at the moment, thank you—we're not ready to order your delicious fares just yet. We're awaiting guests.

MOTHER: And here they are!

Angeles's parents, Miles and Cassandra, arrive without her. The two women air-kiss while the men shake hands.

MOTHER: Cassandra! How wonderful to see you!

CASSANDRA: The pleasure's all mine, Vivian! You look simply wonderful!

MOTHER: As do you, my dear!

FATHER: Good to see you, Miles.

MILES: Put her there, Norman! I've been hearing from head office all day about your great work! Absolutely superb! First rate! Well done!

FATHER: I live to serve the party, Miles. You know me, one for blue and blue for all.

They sit.

MOTHER: So where's Angeles?

CASSANDRA (Looks despondent): She couldn't make it—

SHANA: Thank fuck.

The civilized parents try desperately not to notice this abrasive language.

CASSANDRA: She's revising terribly hard.

MILES: Yes, I think she's really going to crack these exams.

CASSANDRA: How about you, Shana? How is your revision going?

SHANA: Haven't done any—I don't give a fuck about exams.

FATHER: She's quietly confident, aren't you, dear?

SHANA: I might not even bother to go to them—that's how much I give a shit about them.

MOTHER: We've come back tonight to give her a boost—give her that winning push to see her through.

FATHER: We'll revise tonight and she'll come out trumps in the exams, isn't that right, darling?

SHANA: Eat shit.

FATHER: Right, I think I'm ready for the menus. Miles? Cassandra?

The parents nod in agreement and the waiter is sent for.

CASSANDRA: You know, Vivian, the tickets to see the New Young Pony Club arrived in the post this morning.

MOTHER: Superb.

SHANA: The New what?!

MOTHER: The New Young Pony Club—they were a very hip band when we were growing up, dear—very cool—very chic—and they've just recently reformed for a reunion tour. It features lots of neo-pop bands of the noughties.

SHANA: Sounds thrilling.

CASSANDRA: Oh, it'll be just divine.

MILES: That reminds me, Norman—the Moose Teak billiard room chairs arrived at last. I'll drop them off in the morning.

FATHER: First rate, Miles! Nothing will tie together the room more than the Moose Teak. I've been anticipating their arrival with much enthusiasm. This is splendid news.

Shana gets a buzz on her iPalm.

MOTHER: Darling, you really should turn that off at the dinner table.

Shana throws her middle finger up and checks her iPalm.

There is a message from Angeles: 'Enjoying your dinner, bitch!?' Shana texts back: 'Fucking whore!'

FATHER: So what do you think you'll have, Shana!?

SHANA: I'll have the eat-shit burger! I'm out of here.

MOTHER: Okay, darling! Have a wonderful evening! Love you!

<u>7:40 p.m - ANGELES</u>

I remember three years ago when my family and Shana's family all went on holiday together to Norway in the summer. It seemed like the longest holiday ever.

We went by ferry as my parents thought it would be quaint—Shana and I managed to avoid each other for the whole journey (some three days). She found corners and holes to sit in and read her dumb books on various loser philosophers while I found a ship boyfriend—a guy three years older than me, on his gap year from school—you have to be very rich to do that now.

Just before we hit the fjords I let him screw me on the vintage virtual tennis court—he chose the avatar of some random old American player called Jan Michael-Gambil (hot-looking guy) and I chose a Euro-Eastern chick called Daniela Hantuchova.

After he beat me 6-0, he took me on the grass by the net. He was deep, hard, powerful. We were just about to finish up when Shana's mother burst in through the door and told me that dinner would be at seven o'clock, not eight o'clock tonight. She didn't even bat an eyelid, and after she was gone we finished up.

At dinner she talked to me about the future of fashion and said that she was really proud of me for following my dreams, and that Shana should follow her dreams if she had any.

All through dinner, Shana read her book on futurism and shot evil glances at her mother.

I remember seeing the fjords and thinking how beautiful they were—all like tall perfect bodies.

The trip was educational: Bergen was interesting—very hip, Tromso had a ghostly charm, and Oslo was choice. I really like the Norwegian style—they know how to carry themselves and how to dress properly.

We spent a lot of our time going from small town to small town and staying in country villas. I listened to a lot of music. Fortunately, Shana was in a different car to mine so I didn't have to see her.

I remember when we were at a farmhouse, she would love spending time with the chickens and she was the one who had to get the eggs for breakfast. She used to tell the chickens she was sorry for taking their young.

We flew back to England instead of taking the ferry; Shana cried throughout the whole flight.

7:46 p.m - DNA MATLOCK

Somebody called Son of Ellis has posted on Mugbook: 'People in Felixstowe are afraid to merge.'

7:47 p.m - PC MAX RAYBURN—ON PATROL

It's 8:00 p.m. and I'm on patrol—doing the usual tour of Felixstowe's hotspots. It's one year on from the Treetops killings—two girls were abducted there and murdered one week after the other—and we still have no leads.

The killer left traces of fir on the victims, which led to him being called the Fir Man. It shook the area.

We've exhausted all our leads but are still supposed to be in a state of heightened alarm—looking for anything or anybody that looks suspicious.

The shops and buildings down Hamilton Road look sleepy tonight. I sometimes look back at my great grandfather's books about how it was when Felixstowe first started out as a town—it looked much better in black-and-white photos.

7:50 p.m - CYNTHIA CARPATHIAN—BEDROOM

I feel like a dead old man who's been made to live another ten years and he knows he's got to live in agonising pain for those years—that's how I feel.

I switch through the TV channels—not much. The travel channel has its vintage week showing old *Globe Trekkers* featuring that cockney guy and some girl called Megan.

These days the Cockney accent seems to be dying out. At one point my parents said that people who went to London used to put on London accents in order to get on—now they put on American accents to fit in—funny old world, eh?

On the politician channel, Osiris Ferry is holding a press conference to announce his leadership of the New Human Party.

He's saying he'll hold firm to their beliefs in alternative thinking and remaining beyond centre—meaning he doesn't accept that they sit anywhere ordinary on the political spectrum but instead they are 'beyond it.' He keeps going on about the Outersphere, he looks glazed, reeling.

As he goes on to explain this, his eyes start to grow wider and more intense. Ferry has done well for the NHP and a lot of what he says makes sense. I hope he wins—I'd vote but I can't be bothered—I only ever really do anything if I have to.

I try to go back to sleep but I think the amphetamines and cola I've been drinking have finally kicked in and I'm actually even feeling mildly optimistic about going out tonight—but I haven't been out of the house in three weeks so I'm also anxious. I decide the best thing to do is take more amphetamines—so I take several more and hopefully that will swing the positivity and optimism over and above the dread thought of stepping outside.

8:00 p.m - ARNOLD—TOWN CENTRE

I'm hanging with the rest of the F-troop connection outside the Golden Panda Chinese restaurant.

There's benches just across from it so we often sit here, spit rhymes, talk about what we need to talk about, think about the future, and order food when we get hungry.

Some of the boys ain't out tonight due to exams tomorrow but the hard-core are representing correctly.

There's Two-Tone Tony (TTT or Triple T as he's known)—we call him that because we don't know whether he's black or white. He's one of them in-betweeners. T's tight with the rhymes though. Then there's Fat-Ass Larry. He's one dude who could do with leaving the Chinese food alone—permanently.

It seems like we've been doing the same thing for way too long now—just an endless circle of school (kicked that into touch though), Ninsega, listening to the latest tunes, coming up with new rhymes, and kicking it on the bench here. Sure, there's a few parties here and there where we DJ and spit some rhymes but it's not enough. I've had it with this fucking town. As soon as this summer is over I'm out of here—fuck knows where—but I'm going...Malaysia, Saigon, maybe?

8:03 p.m - ANDERSON MARR—BEDROOM

I'm in my room, lying on my imported Japanese yoga mat—doing my breathing exercises—visualizing my exam success tomorrow—going through every stage of the plan—imagining every motion—every possible action I can take and every possible reaction—visualizing my walking in, sitting down, and the successful completion of the exam. I visualize my fellow exam students and their actions and reactions to my success. I consider every probability and within those probabilities my ability to gain success from it. I factor in all scenarios: breathing in—breathing out—relaxing every muscle in my body one at a time—tensing—then relaxing—part by part—seeing my future at an elite Ivy League university and then my subsequent financial services success after that.

I think of all these things and the confidence within me grows. I'm determined to be successful. I finish my routine—drink some mineral water and sit in my contemplation chair.

I look around at my wall of inspiration—I see my financial heroes—the quotes that make a difference—'Whether you think you can or you can't, you're right'—'See your future—be your future.'

I focus on my financial projections forecast. I look at the bar chart that shows my future financial success and I allow myself a smile.

8:11 p.m - MARTHA—GROSVENOR PUBLIC HOUSE

So I'm at the Grosvenor with all the others—having a few drinks before the pillow party starts. The invite said eight but nothing really happens before ten, and everybody needs a neutral territory to unwind and ease out before they fuck each other's brains out—so the Grosvenor seemed like a good option.

We've been coming to the Grosvenor since I can remember—it's our local—everybody who's ever been to our school would consider it as their local—my dad and probably his dad came here—it's a rite of passage and it's filled with lots of different generations reminiscing and wondering where it all went wrong.

Anyway, the pub is heating up: Trudie, Kevin, Subway, Coca-Cola, Karen, Herman, Homebase, Gary, BT, Mary, Pizza Hut, and Kathryn are already here and have moved on from pints to shots. They're drinking the new Absolut Absinthe.

Trudie is saying she's worried that her vagina is too dry to fuck tonight. Homebase tells her not to worry and that Rudolphio has loads of lubes and lotions that will smooth her right out.

Mary says she's brought her own lubes; Gary says how great it is that everyone can now fuck each other bareback and not worry about getting diseases or making each other pregnant—'Can you imagine, back in our parents' day—they had to wear condoms, take pills and still you could get AIDS or get pregnant!

MARY: I knew a guy who got AIDS once, I was on holiday in Spain—he was my holiday boyfriend and he didn't tell me until the end of the holiday. It was on our last night. He said he had AIDS once. He said he just went to his doctor when his dick started burning, the doc gave him the jab, and he was right as rain. It's like wow, can you imagine life without free sex!? It's probably for that reason why our parents are so bloody square! They don't understand this free society that we live in, they're caught up! Repressed! Shackled in their own conservative bloody shit!

HERMAN: All I know is I want a blowjob from whoever sucked me off last time! Man! That girl could suck!

HOMEBASE: How do you know it was a girl?

HERMAN: Come on, man, I was fingering her and grabbing her titties while she did it!

KEVIN: You're nasty, man!

PIZZA HUT: I heard Rudolphio's got a great idea to do something a bit different tonight. I hear he's gonna get us to wear masks of ex-prime ministers!? Now call me fucked up, but that's pretty sick!

MARY: He's a Young Tory, that's why! The guy's got a thing about Cameron—idolises him. I think this way he gets to fuck him in a socially acceptable way.

COCA-COLA: Pretty sick if you ask me!

HERMAN: Man, I hope I get to be George Osbourne.

MARTHA: You think Rudolphio's gay then?

MARY: Don't know, don't care, but the dude throws the best pillow parties in town—good food, drink, drugs, lots of space—his parents are always away—it's perfect.

GARY: Yeah, his parties are pretty awesome. It's just when he gets us to start reciting Young Tory mantras—there's just something wrong there—something not quite right—you know what I mean—all those toasts to Blue Power and the way he turns away anybody wearing red—it's just a bit much, man.

KAREN: It's his parents, dude—they fucked him up on that shit at a very early age—filled his mind with Young Tory crap—spoon-fed him.

GARY: How would you know?

KAREN: Do you remember in junior school when he used to throw shitfits when anybody wore red? I remember he threw a total eppy when someone drew in red on the electric whiteboard. He got up out of his seat and started beating on this poor kid—calling him socialist scum! He was going to get suspended but his parents intervened and smoothed it over.

COCA-COLA: Paid off the school you mean?

KAREN: Anyway, you've just got to understand that there's a reason why he's that way—like any of us who are fucked up are the way we are—it's our parents, dude. They fucked us all up.

GARY: They certainly fucked me up—at least that's what my neurologist says.

BT: They definitely fucked me up.

SIDNEY: And me.

KAREN: Anyway, that's why we do what we do, right? That's why we get so high, drink so much, fuck so much, party so much! It's to get away from what our parents made us—to escape—rise above it.

KEVIN: I'll drink to that!

HOMEBASE: Fuck yeah!

KAREN: Everybody, raise your glasses! Here's to liberation! We're on the brink—the very brink of escape—all we need to do is stay on track for two more weeks—get our asses to that bullshit exam hall for two weeks, that's all, just two little weeks—recycle all the bullshit that they've pumped into us—just write down all the answers they've prepared and fed into us for months and months—let it come out of our heads onto the page—and that's it—we all get our A*s, the school looks good and they all get more funding and results bonuses, and our parents are happy—and they send us off to the States where we're finally fucking free from their talons—free from their bullshit! Free at fucking last! Free at fucking last, bitches! (Everyone laughs.) So I propose this toast to two weeks, my friends! Two weeks is all we need to remember when we're in that stupid fucking place! Two weeks, my motherfuckas!

The group raise their glasses and drink deeply.

KEVIN: Oh shit, look who it is.

Angeles is coming toward them accompanied by Warp Hindrance-Thomas.

SUBWAY: Oh fuck.

KAREN: Everybody, just stay calm—resist the urge to punch her out! We've only got to last fourteen more days with her and then she's gone out of our lives. Two weeks, remember—it's a great mantra to live by.

KEVIN: What are you? Tory now?

Angeles comes over to greet them all.

ANGELES: Well, hello, everybody! And how are we this evening?

MARTHA: Yeah, we're fine, Angeles, how are you?

ANGELES: I'm just great, thank you—wow, Karen! That's a lovely dress! And Coca-Cola, that tiara is just marvellous—a gift from your sponsors perhaps? Oh and Bethany, where did you get those boots?

BETHANY: I got them from—

ANGELES (Interrupting): How delightful, you must be really pleased with your purchase!

BETHANY: Well, actually, I—

ANGELES: Did you?! Wow, how wonderful for you! Really, that is so, so, so...

WARP: Special?

ANGELES: Yes, thank you, Warp, special, that's exactly the word I was looking for...So are we all getting ready for Rudolphio's little pillow party tonight?

HOMEBASE: Yeah, we're going, if that's what you mean?

ANGELES: Oh—that's so cute, how adorable.

KAREN: What the fuck's that supposed to mean?

ANGELES: Exactly what it sounded like, my dear.

SUBWAY: Are you going, Angeles?

ANGELES: Oh no, I don't think so. Pillow parties were something I did a long time ago—I've grown out of that now.

KAREN: Get fucked, Angeles.

ANGELES: Like you will be tonight, Karen? Do you think someone would want to though? Gosh, I love optimism—good for you!

KAREN: Just take your bullshit pseudo-sophisticated bullshit somewhere else, okay?

ANGELES: Big words from such a big girl—how fitting!

The group holds Karen back.

ANGELES: Oh, I know the truth hurts, Karen—but once you own up to it, then everything will be so much better—you'll learn to live with your contemptible fat ugliness I'm sure—just like I've had to live with being the most stunning human being in this desolate town full of sad reprobates. It's hard work but somebody's got to do it.

KAREN: I'm gonna beat the absolute fuck out of you, you stupid dumb whore!

ANGELES: Such harsh words from such an ugly mouth—they go so well together.

Karen is furious.

COCA-COLA: Get the fuck out of here, Angeles, before I let her go!

ANGELES: Sadly I do have to leave. You see, I find it important to spend time with people of calibre—people of culture—people of standing—people of good breeding. So I bid you good night, children.

BETHANY: Get fucked, Angeles!

Angeles leaves.

KAREN: Oh that bitch! I could kill her, I could really kill her.

SUBWAY: We all could.

MARTHA: You know what, maybe we should?

The group contemplate for a moment.

KEVIN: We could but then we'd go to prison and not be able to drink Absolut Absinthe anymore!

KAREN: Yeah, well, fuck that then! Maybe we'll just cripple her or something.

Elsewhere in the pub: Billy and Tommy are sinking pints and talking about the weekend.

BILLY: Man, it's gonna be a hot summer! Tiffany Young's new game comes out.

TOMMY: Yeah, man! It'll be one long wet summer! Man, did you hear?! My copy of *Ass Sluts 2* arrived the other day and I got the new anal interface for it!

BILLY: Anal interface!? What the fuck is that?

TOMMY: Dude, it's great! It's basically a big butt. I ordered a black one, but you can get them in different shades of white, black, yellow, etc...It's great—it's just like the vagina interface except you just fuck the butt instead.

BILLY: Has it got the same Cum-Clean Collect System?

TOMMY: Yup—new and improved though. The new suction system cleans up everything, man! No nasty little surprises for you the next time you use it.

BILLY: Cool, man! Yeah, that does get a bit nasty, not to mention uncomfortable and probably not very hygienic either.

TOMMY: This one has a lotion you put in it that cleans everything out properly. But check it out though—it was delivered the other day—but my parents intercepted the package. They were suspicious so they opened it up and of course they found this fucking big black butt right there!

BILLY: Oh man! What the fuck did they do!?

TOMMY: Well, they didn't know what it was at first! I said it was a mistake, that I never ordered anything like that, that it must've been a mistake! You know, SuperNet pirates tapping me up for something I didn't pay for.

BILLY: Right, so what happened?

TOMMY: Well, they phoned up the company—found out that my eurocard had ordered it! They almost killed me!

BILLY: What did they do with it?

TOMMY: Tossed it, man! They found all my porn games too and threw them out too! Then they confiscated my eurocard and told me to go out and find real girls. Then they talked to me about the dangers of anal sex—something about diseases you can get from it? I was like, what?! Get with the times, dudes!

BILLY: Real girls? Man! Who needs real girls?! They're so yesterday.

TOMMY: I know right, plus you have to talk to them and buy them shit and stuff, right?

BILLY: Yeah, that's no good—and what girl can even dream of looking as good as Tiffany Young?

TOMMY: Exactly! And they won't always put out! It's frustrating, man! Whereas I know with *Suck and Fuck: Gold Edition* that I'm gonna get a kick-ass blowjob from a good-looking whore and then I'm gonna blow my load in her doggy style, all in the comfort of my own room—and I can do that whenever I want!

BILLY: Sex on tap.

TOMMY: Exactly, bro—and we're horny young dudes with needs! All this exam pressure! We need a release! It's not like using drugs. It's healthy, it's time efficient, and it's cheap! It's what we need after a hard day of revision, dude!

BILLY: Exactly—if only they saw some sense. So, man, what are you going to do without all your porn?

TOMMY: Well, check this out! I went to the trash-bin to get it all back—you know, at like 2:00 a.m.—the day before the trash guy came—and guess what—it'd gone, right!?

BILLY: No!? What fucka would take that?!

TOMMY: I don't know, right. So anyway, I'm pissed off the next day at school, so I come home early—and I find my dad's car parked and I go in the back door and there's all this noise coming from upstairs—so I creep upstairs and I can hear the noise is coming from my dad's bedroom!

BILLY: No!?

TOMMY: Yup! I take a sneak peek and there he is on his knees—naked on his bed—*Ass Sluts 2* playing on his Greenscreen 3000—and he's giving it hard to the black butt anal interface—slapping on the butt and screaming, 'That's it, Yolanda! Take my big white cock right up your shitter! That's it, you whore! That's it! You love it, you slut!' So, I'm half disgusted, half-pissing myself—and then right when he comes, he turns around and sees me watching and I just run out of the house!

BILLY: Ahhh, no way, man! No way! How did you deal with that!?

TOMMY: Well, I didn't—I spent the whole day away from the house—found any excuse not to be there—but eventually I get a text from my dad saying he wants to talk—so I meet him and I don't know what to say! There's a moment of silence and then he just comes right out and hugs me. He says, 'That game's the greatest thing in the world,' and he makes a deal with me! He tells me where he's hiding the butt and my porn games and tells me I can use them when no one's around, as long as I promise not to tell my step-mother.

BILLY: Oh my god! Grossss! So what?! You're gonna share it with him?

TOMMY: Sure, why not!? It's better than not having it at all—we've both promised we'll wash our cocks before we play and use the cleansing function after and keep it superclean. I've also promised to give him some of the cheats—so he can get to the end-of-level whores—and he's given me a new eurocard with an increased limit. Plus, I can't stand my step-mother, so it's kind of a revenge!

BILLY: I know, dude, but oh my god!? Your dad!? With his dick in the same place where yours has been?! Ewww! I think I'm gonna throw up!

TOMMY: It's not that bad really. I mean, think about it—I've come from his sperm anyway, so it's more or less the same.

BILLY: Awwww, man! That's just soooo wrong!

TOMMY: Well, like I said, at least this time I get to use it and don't have to bother trying to be all nice and boyfriendly to the whores in here!

BILLY: You know that! They act like they don't want it—but they do!

Martha walks by.

TOMMY: Hi, Martha.

MARTHA: Hi, Tommy. So are you guys going to the pillow party tonight?

TOMMY (To Billy): Did you get an invite?

BILLY: No, you?

TOMMY: No.

MARTHA: Too bad, guys, it's gonna rock!

BILLY: Who needs real sex, right?

TOMMY: Yeah, we've got Tiffany!

BILLY: Yeah!

MARTHA: Whatever.

Martha walks back over to the others.

MARTHA: I feel sorry for Billy and Tommy.

HOMEBASE: So you all got dollars on you?

KAREN: Why?

HOMEBASE: Well, you know there's going to be dog there right? Sex on dog is the best.

BIG MAC: I might go down to the Spa Gardens to get mine.

HOMEBASE: Man, you must be joking! They'll rip you off down there! No! Trust me, Ruben's promised me some good stuff, save your money for later.

BIG MAC: I'm going to the Spa Gardens—anybody coming with me?

Head shakes all round.

HOMEBASE: Man, you must be crazy going down there—especially alone—you're nuts, dude.

BIG MAC: Man, whatever, I'll see you at the party, dude. And yo! Bethany! Make sure you wear the George Osbourne mask—I want to know how to find you!

BETHANY: You got it, lover boy!

HOMEBASE: He's crazy. They're animals down there in the Spa!

KEVIN: Ahh, man! You're only saying that 'cause they kicked your ass last summer.

HOMEBASE: I just took one of their dumbbells—it was no big deal—they totally overreacted!

KEVIN: Yeah, but you should know better! Those Spa meatheads are pretty fond of their dumbbells.

MARTHA: Sure—without their dumbbells they've got no identity—they wouldn't know what to do with themselves!

HOMEBASE: I still say he's crazy! Rudolphio's's got the hook-up—why bother risking shit with those loony fucknuts!?

KAREN: You say Rudolphio's got the hook-up? You sure it's as good as you say it is?

HOMEBASE: Absofuckinglutely.

KEVIN: Cool, okay then, man, cos mixing dog with Viagra makes my johnson very very happy!

JUDITH: Makes my vag pretty ecstatic too!

KEVIN: Okay, I'm going to the EasyBank to get some credits out—make sure you secure me one, yeah, Homebase.

HOMEBASE: No worries, dude.

JUDITH: I'll come too—gotta check my credit balance.

Coca-Cola is in a dazed and dreamlike state—looking up at the sky.

MARTHA: You okay, Coke?

COCA-COLA: The summer is like a hideously offensive illusion, isn't it? It's built up as this thing of beauty when really it's actually the arbiter of death—because what comes after summer? Winter—and what does winter mean? Death. Summer is merely a harbinger of death.

MARTHA: What about autumn then? Doesn't that come first?

COCA-COLA: Autumn's made-up, it doesn't really exist.

MARTHA: Spring?

COCA-COLA: A fallacy. There are really only two seasons and they're both bad.

8:25 p.m - KENNETH—SEAFRONT

I'm absolutely fucked on some acid called Red Ohms and all I can think is:

Dreamy hazy superlative creamy skies—unicorns riding delicately on their whims—the soft skipping of melting fruit baskets gusseting the plum men as they go about their duties. The next levels are shifting and grooving, finding their way onward. The ground shakes smoothly and tells us of its belief in us. It wants us to journey inward—to find Xaaltha.

8:30 p.m - DNA MATLOCK—BEDROOM

I'm sitting here at home, thinking 'Why the fuck am I sitting here at home revising for my happiness exam tomorrow?!' I'm revising the question on serotonin and how it relates to food, and how eating certain foods like nuts, bananas, and fish can make you happy, or how you can just take the government's M pill and get all these ingredients in one happy combination. I take M every day—but I don't think it makes me any happier.

If the government wants us all to be happy, then why do they make us sit stupid exams about being happy? Why don't they just let us get on with our lives and not have to sit stupid spoon-fed exams.

When I think about the future it's quite depressing. It just seems like all I've done since I was five is study, revise, write assignments, go to revision or assignment clubs, get tested, get assessed, and repeat. How the fuck can I be happy about that!?

Sometimes I wish I was like the dropouts, the people who say fuck it and just quit. It seems like more and more sense to me—and maybe I will—maybe after I take these exams, I'll say fuck it to the university entrance exams and drop out.

DNA'S MOTHER (From downstairs): Son! Did you remember to take your learning pill?

DNA: Yes, Mother.

DNA'S MOTHER: Good lad, I'll remind you when it's time to take the next one. Oh, and that nice Mr. Vandermark called and said not to forget that the question weighting on the third part of the happiness exam as it's going to be heavily focused on neurotransmitters. So just make sure you've got it covered.

DNA: Thanks, mum, yes, mum, I've got it covered.

DNA'S MOTHER: Happy studying!

DNA: Happy…Mmm…

9:00 p.m - ANDERSON MARR—HOME

I'm finishing up my evening preparation. I let the badger out for some playtime in his garden pen and watch him as he moves around. Current studies have proven that watching animals at play is good for soothing the soul—something that is not lost on me. Any last-minute soothing will leave me relaxed and settled—enabling me to sleep deeply and regenerate my brain cells, muscles, and cardiovascular system in preparation for tomorrow's victory.

The badger mooches around—sniffing at this and that—munching some food every now and again. He probes the pen's defences. The pen is strong but he has been able to escape from its confines before. My parents got him several years ago when badgers were the new pet accessory to have. Since then, their popularity has dwindled, something that I thought would happen—that's why I never invested shares in them.

Several minutes later and I am content that he will not escape so I leave him to enjoy his solitude while I check the stocks and shares report, *The Kaiserooney Report* on Bloomberg. This is my favourite show as it has an analyst whose predictions I rate and have followed for some time—leading me to make a lot of money from his sage counsel.

I munch some zero-fat soya crisps and drink mineral water as he goes on to explain that the third and fourth quarter of this year will be a time for very cautious optimism and he reiterates the need to think carefully about our future investments and to plan concisely for next year. I take notes on my iPalm.

9:59 p.m - HARRISON—SECURE RUBBER ROOM—HOSPITAL

Harrison bounces off the walls while dribbling ferociously.

HARRISON: Boohhjjjjjj! Yuckateeeee! Yuckateeeeeeee!!

10:00 p.m - CYNTHIA CARAPTHIAN—HOME

I'm on my doorstep and have been trying to step out of the house for the last thirty minutes—the amphetamines have done their job and the Coke Plus helped to—but every time I take a step out I just want to retract that step—I don't know what to do—so I decide the addition of alcohol could give me the push I need—so I go to the lounge—get the rum and add it to the Coke. I take several big gulps and several more and wait...

10:05 p.m - CHRIS—NEW ALLENBY PARK

We walk in through the entrance of New Allenby Park. This dark stretch of path is adorned with old overhanging oak trees and decorative foliage.

Dim torchlight can be seen in the distance. The alley smells of cheap vodka, fetid dog shit, and bracken. My eight-man crew raise and twirl their umbrellas as we stroll serenely in unison. We alternate kicking our legs up in the air with raising our knees up. It's a bizarre walk-dance that I designed to beguile, perturb, and disturb opponents. It's a tactic I developed after reading about Shock and Awe in a book on military strategy.

We begin to sing, 'Knees up mother brown, knees up mother brown, knees up, knees up, knees up, knees up—'cause we're gonna kick your fucking heads in!'

The lines of dog we did in Butchy's garage seem to have got the boys suitably revved up, that and the bottles of brandy we consumed.

Some people wonder why I do this? Why do this crazy shit when I could just be a good student. I'm predicted all A**s. They say, 'Why risk your future of Harvard?'

I've already had several police cautions—and some say I've already blown it, but to tell you the truth, I don't care.

It seems pretty obvious to me that this bullshit world has no meaning, no purpose, no point.

Religion, the state, the family, education, behaving—they all exist only because someone had the balls to make them exist. They fought their way into our existence. Existence can just as easily be pummelled into the shape you want it to take.

I don't have to abide by society's rules: I make my own. I'm the leader of the Black Hatters because I like power; I like violence because I get pleasure from inflicting pain and because it's visceral and real with no pretensions or falsities. I enjoy getting hurt because it confirms my existence; I drink brandy and take dog because they elevate my mood; I like girls but don't go out of my way to attain them because they can be an imposition; I go to school because I find teachers amusing; I'll go to Harvard because I want to experience the novelty of it and the gift of the new is a prize worth pursuing.

So I live within this so-called society, but believe me, I am a whole different world within it.

As my man Captain Kierkegaard said, 'The highest and most beautiful things in life are not to be heard about, nor read about, nor seen but, if one will, are to be lived.'

I look around me as my hit squad advances. Johnny Jackrabbit is on my right-hand side. He's in year eleven—a solid fighter, average student, just recently he's becoming a little too fond of the dog.

Further on the right are Tim and Harvey—in year ten, green, but eager to prove themselves and proving to be great dog-dealers. On my extreme left: Butchy, a big burly year-thirteen drop-out—he was never going to last, his bad grades would bring the school down, so they trumped up some bullshit charges and kicked him out. Now Butchy spends his days selling dog for us, intimidating locals, and watching old Westerns.

By him is Anthony, another dropout, very short chap. Next to me are: Sven, a Norwegian exchange student who fell into our clutches, and Tommy Rightway, a grade-fourteen who I'm unsure about, and that's exactly why he's here tonight.

I'm confident: the Warthog number somewhere between ten to eleven members but I doubt all of them were brave enough to make it out tonight. We've beaten the shit out of the Warthogs in our previous four rumbles (all under my leadership). Several of them suffered broken bones and one of them is in intensive care.

They've found it hard to generate new members after such consistent humiliation but then again, they're stupid and have nothing better to do than get into fights.

I can see them now: they're by one of the goalposts. The glow from their zap sticks is a giveaway. I refuse to let my boys fight with zap sticks—they're an odious and bourgeois invention that leave no room for finesse. With an umbrella you can do a number of weird and wonderful things: batter your opponent, shield a kick or punch from view, and perform interesting dances to boot. It's the weapon of choice for the sophisticated thug and adds a touch of style to our noble coterie.

We line up a few dozen metres away from them. They're waving their zap sticks and chanting taunts and insults—they're unorganized, not dispersed in any particularly strategic way—this doesn't surprise me as the Treeman was the only one who had any brains in their organisation and he's in a coma.

There's only about nine of them—they haven't got a chance—they're hesitant—not sure now whether they should be here—not sure whether they're up to it.

They're thinking about home: Skyvision, the SuperNet, drinking tea, being in bed, being anywhere but here. I can sense it, I can smell it, and I love it—inflicting pain on those in fear is so satisfying.

I know exactly how to deploy my boys: 'Gentlemen—Preston Pans!'

Immediately, my boys form a tight line. Preston Pans is my code for a tactic used by the Highlanders against the English army in 1745. It relies on speed, strength, shock and awe, and more importantly: fear. It's just a savage charge really and it's right up my alley. A classic implementation of Shock and Awe.

'All right boys! This is it! Highland charge!'

We rush at them: umbrellas closed, the tips pointing out—ready to ram into them. They hold their ground and we're on them—I ram my umbrella into one about my own age. He falls back onto the floor and I start whacking him with the umbrella handle. His eyes shut and he offers no more resistance (unconscious, bluffing, or dead?).

I look around me: Butchy has one by the throat and is choking him. I hear the sound and smell of zap stick on flesh and turn to see Tommy Rightway zapped to the floor.

I take a huge swing and whack the offending Warthog to the ground and start pounding on his head.

Around me the balance of the fight is still in progress, then there is a cry from one of the Hoggers:

'Now, boyz!'

Suddenly, from all around us, scores of hidden assailants come from the bushes and are on us! Some have zap sticks, some are without, but there's too many and we are quickly overrun.

An interesting turn of events but a disaster nonetheless, a strategic withdrawal is now necessary.

'Dunkirk!' I cry out and my boys try to shake off their attackers. The plan now consists of getting to the cars garrisoned outside the park.

Several of the Warthogs are trying to hold me while a zap sticker approaches intently.

I use my long fingernails to gouge at their eyes and they scream in pain. Their grips released, I make for the cars—I look to see Anthony still fighting. He swings and hits a Warthogger—flattening him—but he doesn't see a zap sticker come at him from behind—Anthony's fried.

Sven is also down and receiving a kicking. Butchy is running next to me as we are pursued but I can't see the others.

10:15 p.m - VANDERMARK—THE HOSPITAL

I'm at the madhouse and I'm going to try to break Harrison out of here. He's essential for my campaign to steer the school back into the black. If we don't get good results, then I'm finished and most likely the school will be absorbed by the Academies Trust. That can't happen so I'll do anything to make sure our numbers add up. I've already recruited some 'ringer' students—scholars from local schools who are standout academics.

I've enrolled them and fixed it so that it appears they were here from the start of the year. I had to pay a hacker, some Korean character I met online, quite a considerable sum of money to do this—but he's the best and he assured me that they'll never be able to tell or trace the fixing back to me or him—I hope that's the case as this little indiscretion has made quite a big dent in next year's school budget.

There's five of them and they'll sit the exam tomorrow and will substantially alter the predicted results for the school's happiness quotient. That will result in a higher budget for the school next year and a significant pay increase for me.

I climb over the outer fencing—using a smart-ladder I bought earlier. I hide the smart ladder in the bushes and move stealthily across the grass—edging toward the entrance—I can see Harrison through the big reinforced plasti-glass bay windows in the rest area. He's sitting on the carpet and smacking himself in the head with something.

I sidle toward the outer exit but it's locked; I'm about to explore another way in when I hear voices and a dog bark. I quickly run off and make for the wall—I'll just have to hope the ringers are enough to get me back into our projected success ratio.

10:25 p.m - CHRIS—BUTCHY'S GARAGE

We're in Butchy's garage—nursing our wounds—it went bad, no doubt about that. The Hogs have more savvy that I thought. They must have a new leader or partner—someone who actually knows what they're doing—someone with enough smarts to come up with an ambush. I must do some intelligence on this new and improved outfit and find their weaknesses. Meanwhile bourbon and dog are doing the job of numbing our pain and restoring our spirits.

I'm comforted by one of the K-man's great lines:

'Trouble is the common denominator of living. It is the greatest equalizer.'

I look around at the remnants of my army: of the remainder, the two young ones, Tim and Harvey, are most keen to track the Warthogs down and kill them—probably because they're the most hopped up on drugs.

The others have had enough—they make their excuses and leave—I'm in no mood to punish them tonight—I'll think of some suitable retribution at a later stage—those absent, the beaten and bruised, I also excuse. I am going out on a solo mission tonight—into the darkness—into uncertainty, into the void, into possible oblivion. Sounds splendid...

<u>11:00 p.m - SHANA—THE HORROR BOX</u>

So I'm in the Horror Box night club. It's eleven and some bore called Martin is drivelling into my ear.

MARTIN: So I ask myself, am I happy being honest—being absolutely candid? Or was I happier when I was deceptive and was not who I appeared to be? I mean, does the relief of unburdening match the pleasure of a safety barrier? I honestly can't tell?

SHANA: I think you shouldn't be happy either way as no matter what choice you make, you'll still be incredibly ugly.

Martin looks forlorn and trundles off.

<u>11:05 p.m - FREYA—HOME</u>

It's late and I'm word-voicing my application to NYU—and I feel cold even though it's warm so I make myself some coffee—but then I decide to drink tea instead because tea is nicer—so I make myself tea and immediately I feel better—I raid my parents' cupboards and find some real biscuits and start to binge—in ten minutes time it'll all be going down the toilet.

11:28 p.m - MARSHALL—HOME

I'm sitting in my parent's conservatory getting high and freaking myself out—listening to the Sleepy Jackson—an Aussie group from the noughties—the song's called 'Devil Was in My Garden' and it's very appropriate as I'm starting to get very paranoid. I have a problem when I get high where sometimes I think I'm going to explode—spontaneously combust—I don't remember when it first happened but it happens way too much.

I'll be sitting round a friend's house or in a car getting stoned somewhere, when all of a sudden I'll start to panic—then I'll think about the documentary I saw about people who spontaneously combust and then I'll start thinking—oh shit! It's going to happen to me, isn't it—I'm going to explode!

And then I start to play the scenario out in my head—me exploding and getting all guts and blood and bone all over my friend's parents' living room—and them having to try and clean it up and having to explain to the police and their parents and my parents about it. 'Oh sorry, Mr. McGregor, but we were just getting stoned—nothing weird—just normal synthetic sinsemilla, when your son exploded into pieces in front of us—I'm really sorry about that—we didn't really mean it—didn't plan it or anything. It was just one of those things. Just one of those spontaneous combustion things.'

So then I think, shit! I can't let this happen in this room! Firstly, it would be really embarrassing and I'd never hear the end of it, and secondly my friends and family would be upset and no doubt pissed off—so I leave.

I'm hoping that if I get home and go to bed and explode there it will be much better and less suspect as people die in their sleep all the time, so what's to stop them from blowing up in their sleep?

So, with this in mind, I head back to my home and climb into bed—my heart rate pounding and my pulse going nuts. My head feels like it'll be the first to go with the blood vessel by my temple seemingly about to burst—I try to shut my eyes and see it out—thinking that this won't hurt much—and then thankfully somehow I finally manage to get to sleep and that's that.

<u>11:30 p.m - RUDOLPHIO—RUDOLPHIO'S HOUSE PARTY</u>

My party is in full flow but the masks have not yet made an appearance as nobody is horny enough. They are waiting for the dog to mix with the Viagra.

There is a ring at the door—this must be my man. I open the door to see a bruised and battered Chris.

CHRIS: Good evening.

RUDOLPHIO: Shit the bed, man! What happened to you?

CHRIS: Had a little tumble with a few of the Warthog fellas—how's the party going?

RUDOLPHIO: Yeah all right, but it'll go a lot better with what I hope you've brought.

CHRIS: You have the credits.

RUDOLPHIO: In full, please step into my office.

CHRIS: Can't do that, old friend, I've got business to attend to.

Chris hands Ruben an envelope with the dog and Ruben hands him an envelope of eurocredits.

CHRIS: Much obliged.

RUDOLPHIO: You sure you won't stay? Should be a wild party.

CHRIS: I appreciate the offer, chap, but like I said, I've got business.

RUDOLPHIO: You'd make a good politician, you know that, Chris. We're looking for people like you. I bet you're a great chess player.

CHRIS: Funny you should say that as, 'I feel as if I were a piece in a game of chess, but when my opponent says of it: That piece cannot be moved.'

RUDOLPHIO: Sure, okay...You're a strange guy, Chris, anybody ever tell you that? A bit hard to understand sometimes, know what I mean?

CHRIS: 'People understand me so poorly that they don't even understand my complaint about them not understanding me.'

RUDOLPHIO: Sure, good luck, guy. Be easy.

CHRIS: Enjoy the drugs and fornication. And remember: 'Most men pursue pleasure with such breathless haste that they hurry past it.' Don't make the same mistake, will you?

RUDOLPHIO: Sure, Chris, whatever you say, bro...

Rudolphio closes the door behind him and looks at the big bag of dog with glee. He goes into the main room where the revellers are anxious.

RUDOLPHIO: All right! The dog is here! Let's get this fucking party started!!

The crowd go crazy.

<u>11:45 p.m - ANGELES—THE BOX</u>

So I'm in the Box and I'm wearing the cutest Jervazi dress—purple, to match my purple Gucci top—and my purple Manolo shoes—with purple Nico socks—and I'm carrying my purple Nikono bag—and I'm happy—content even—ready for whatever this evening brings—I'm checking out everybody else's clothes and predictably they're shocking—mismatching and lacking—so very very typical of this tawdry town.

I'm surveying the dance-floor—seeing if there is anybody worth talking to and I'm drawing a big blank—and now Jake Jillovich-Johnson is at the bar with me and he's talking about his dreams of going to Hawaii State University on a surfing scholarship—and I'm saying, 'That's nice,' and he's saying, 'Yeah, dude—it's like my dream—and it's like what I work toward every day—and it's like what I'm going to do—I just know it—all I need to do is win the Cornwall Championship and I'm in—it's like what they say in positivity class—all you gotta do is believe in your dreams and you can achieve anything you want. Anything, dude, like anything. Dude?! Dude!? Are you listening to me or what?!'

I tell him that the fleas in his hair go well with his manky two-year-old shirt and that yes, he'll surely win the championship if the other competitors die of syphilis and then I tell him that I hear Bournemouth University would snap him up and then he's telling me, 'Man, you're so negative—screw you!'

As he leaves, a goal that I had intended, I turn my back on him to look in my bag to find out what the new Mugbook updates are...

Kevin Whinman-Hearne has posted up some stupid videos from Scum.tv; Jarvis Parker is banging on about the pointlessness of existence; and DNA Matlock has claimed that he knows the meaning of existence. He's off his face on his own homemade chemicals again—no doubt. It's a wonder what he can do with a kitchen cupboard.

I post up: 'I'm in the Box and it's boring.' Immediately, Karen says she 'adores' this.

Now I notice someone in his thirties is by my side—and he's trying to look casual—ordering a drink while taking a look at me. I'm intrigued, he looks like he's got money—nice Romani business suit, tie, good shoes. He delivers his opening salvo:

'Every time I come in here I wonder why I did.'

'Why do you then?' I purr casually.

'It's the only place to come at this time of night. So what do you do for a living?'

'I'm still in school.'

'Oh really? Deben or Well-Done?'

'Deben.'

'That's good—I know some kids who go to the Well-Done Academy—and there's something wrong with them—we take some of them for work experience and unless you congratulate and praise them all the time they don't do anything.'

'What line of work are you in?'

'Insurance.'

'How boring. How much do you make?'

'Excuse me?'

'How much do you make? If I'm to continue this conversation, I'd like to know whether you're worth talking to.'

This causes my mystery man to walk away. Some other random, seeing his opportunity, comes up to me and says:

'I have never told anyone this before but…'

'But what?'

'I don't know—I've forgotten.'

11:49 p.m - JEFFREY—BENT HILL

I look up casually at the electric advertisement sign on Bent Hill. It says: 'God has Stan Rusinsky's dog.'

Friday, 16 June

12:02 a.m - ANGELES—THE BOX

I see Cynthia Carpathian—wearing a yellow dress (yellow for fuck's sake!)—she tells me that she's feeling nervous about the exams—which I can understand as she's spent most of this year off with chronic fatigue syndrome—she's been in every now and again but not very often—just to get papers and take them home to study and complete.

It definitely seems to have affected her confidence as she is stuttering and sweating—and she used to be the very picture of cool—I remember a time when she would even try to stick up her nose at me—but I soon sorted that out.

I tell Cynthia that everything is going to be okay and I compliment her on her dress and tell her how wonderful it is and how she will be okay and how she'll get into any university she wants and that yes, we'll go and visit each other and that yes, of course we'll hang out all the time over the summer—and yes, we'll go shopping in London and New York, and yes, I'll help her study—and I kiss her on the cheek and say I have to go and speak to someone *over there* and she says that's funny because she was going to say exactly the same thing.

Then I'm at the bar—ordering a drink—and I see Cynthia standing on her own on the dance floor—looking out at the crowds—visibly shaking—looking like a poor little lost seal who's been abandoned and knows they've only got a few hours left to live—and she tries to make eye contact with some of the people on the dance floor but they're like strangers to her and she tries to meet their gaze but they're like phantoms—unavailable—and now she's dropped her glass on the floor—and it's like it's in slow motion and it smashes dramatically on the floor—exploding all over the floor—going everywhere—and still no one pays her any notice—nobody even bats an eyelid or shrugs—it's like she is destined to be outcast—and now she's crying—sobbing slowly, rooted to the spot with horror and remorse—asking where has her life gone?

She's making a scene but being totally ignored and you can almost see her being swallowed up by dark demons of despair who are enveloping her, cloaking her, smothering her in a wall of invisibility and cutting her off from the real world—she's doomed.

I make a reminder to myself to not ever ever get chronic fatigue syndrome.

Someone comes up to me from behind and says, 'Did you hear about Stan Rusinsky's dog? God has it now, isn't that great.'

1:00 a.m - RUDOLPHIO'S TORY ORGY PILLOW PARTY—KEVIN

The orgy is in full swing. I've got my dick stuck in a girl who has a Peter Mandelson mask on. I'm doing her from behind and this is all while I finger a girl with a Thatcher mask on and suck the tits of a girl with a John Major mask on—wild times!

The dog and Viagra mix has really kicked in and turned us all into sexed-crazed maniacs. There are trays with lines of the purple powder all over Rudolphio's lounge. People take sniff breaks in between their fucking.

The music blaring in the background is *gothic drum and bass future jazz* and the rhythmical thumping sounds go hand in hand with my pumping as I stick it to Mandy!

I think I can see Martha under a George Osbourne mask. She is kneeling beneath two dudes in Mark Farrington-Wright masks as she sucks off one, then the other.

On my left someone, could be a girl, in a Cameron mask, is licking out a girl in a Thatcher mask while she is fucked from behind by a Kenneth Clarke mask.

There's a girl or guy (can't tell) on the couch, wanking off a fat guy (must be Billy) in a Nick Clegg mask as she smokes an e-cigar.

By her side two guys are smothering yoghurt on a girl—all over her—they're layering it on her—then they're licking it off her—one working on her nipples while the other laps at her vagina.

Someone is fucking a girl on the carpet—she is being shuffled across the floor as he does so—they've gone from one side of the room to the other—they hit a table and one of Rudolphio's parents' antique vases smashes on the floor.

'Sorry,' the guy says.

'Hey, no problem, dude! Just keep fucking, guy!' says Rudolphio, and everybody goes back to screwing again.

Someone with a Michael Portillo mask is carrying a tray of Blodka shots.

I take two shots as this stuff is great and it completely accentuates the high. I gargle them. . .Then I kiss Mandy through the rubber and send the liquid through the hole in her mask and down her throat.

There is a sudden barking sound and I turn round to see a little King Charles spaniel dressed up in a George Osbourne mask. It's barking ferociously at everyone. Someone tells it to shut the fuck up. Someone else says:

'Hey, man! I always liked your fiscal policies!'

Someone else picks it up and takes it out of the room.

A girl in a Thatcher mask starts taking photos. I'm concerned but then I realize we're all wearing masks so even if these do end up on Mugbook, they'll be no problem.

Then someone stops the music for a moment and shouts out, 'Isn't this the best fucking party of all time or what!!?'

Someone screams out, 'Yeah!' and everyone starts humping away again.

1:07 a.m - CHRIS—THE HORROR BOX

This place is dark and morbid. The bar is long, sleek, and perfect for steady drinking. The doormen look on edge for some reason—strange for a Thursday. The owner, Sebastien, is behind the bar in his office, looking through papers.

I'm standing at the bar—drinking another double rum and coke with a pinch of dog added in for effect. I'm looking around at the various dribble drabble that infests this nocturnal scratching post—this is the only place in Felixstowe to get a drink after 1:00 a.m. on any day of the week.

For a Thursday it's quite busy—there's a lot of students from my school and the Well-Done Academy are out celebrating the start of the exams tomorrow. Both schools have been force-feeding us the answers so many times now that is doesn't matter what we do to our brains tonight—we'll still be able to go in there tomorrow and regurgitate the answers.

Perhaps that's what makes some of us so cynical—the absurdity and pointlessness of these zero-challenge life tests. I see a girl with a military jacket at the end of the bar—she is making air-knife slits on her arm, Shana, I think her name is.

She looks attractive, cute even, in an angry, militant way. I can tell she is one of the movement, it's obvious, she's so riled up, pent-up with rage about the way things are going in this country, in the world…Poor girl, if only she knew my way. I think about talking to her, but I realize we have nothing in common—she wants to change the world and I want to fuck it.

She would start talking about politics and I would yawn. Instead, I look out onto the dance floor and see two Warthoggers I recognise from the ruck earlier on.

When I've had enough to drink, I'm going to go over there and beat the shit out of them. I am about to order another drink when an attractive young lady walks up and joins me at the bar.

ANGELES: I like your hat.

CHRIS: Thanks. I like your face.

ANGELES: So are you going to buy me a drink?

CHRIS: No, you're going to buy me one.

ANGELES: (To the bartender) Lemolime Daq.

CHRIS: So are you ready to fuck up your exams?

ANGELES: Consider it done, you?

CHRIS: Sure.

I am suddenly grabbed by three bouncers and dragged behind the bar and into the office. My last vision is that of the blond beauty I was speaking to as something is put over my mouth and I lose consciousness.

<u>1:10 a.m - SOMEONE SOMEWHERE</u>

Somebody has just posted this up on Mugbook: 'I have decided to recall myself from the megamarket shelves. I am no longer available for public consumption.'

<u>1:11 a.m - ANGELES—THE BOX</u>

I've just seen Chris dragged away by door staff—who knocked his hat off. I pick it up—it's an Alfred Dunhill—nice, very stylish. I post up the following on Mugbook: 'Chris O'Reilly has just been dragged off by the bouncers at the Horror Box.'

I sip at my Lemdaq—too much lime but oh well, never mind. I turn around to see Shana staring at me with needle eyes, she's nursing a pint of blueberry cider.

ANGELES: What's your problem, bitch?

Shana storms over to me.

SHANA: You've got some nerve, you skank whore!

ANGELES: Why so upset, Shana? Did you happen to look in the mirror again? Always a mistake.

SHANA: I read the thing you said about me on Mugbook.

ANGELES (Surprised): What? But I—

SHANA: But what?! But this, bitch!

Shana throws a fist at me but I am quick and manage to evade it. The bouncers are on Shana immediately and frogmarch her outside. That bitch! Why did she—how did she see that posting?! I deleted it…I check my Mugbook and go back five pages to see that, yes, shit! It's there. Fuck it! Ha! It's quite funny actually!

<u>1:17 a.m - RUPERT—THE BOX</u>

I'm dancing with some guys and gals from the Well-Done Academy. I have a nice dog and vodka buzz going on and am happy but the night is turning strange.

I see Tim in the middle of the dance floor and he's dancing like a happily demented spastic—flailing out his arms everywhere and generally managing to clear the floor of people who are eagerly getting out of his way. I ask him whether he's made a decision to follow God or the devil and he says, 'Neither!—I'm going Buddha, dude! Wooooooooooooo! Buddha baby!!!!!!!!! Yeahhhhhhhhhhh! I'm gonna be a Buddha boy all the way!!!! Wooooooooooooo!!!!!'

At this point he turns and twists and starts to work himself into a dizzying fury until he pukes and falls unconscious on the floor and is dragged out by security.

The door staff is having a busy night and I just catch a glimpse of Chris O'Reilly getting escorted into the back office and then I see Shana decking Angeles! What's gotten into everyone? Must be exam fever! I break off my dance, say good night to everyone, and go to see if Shana is all right.

Outside she is shouting and screaming at the bouncers who remain implacable. She keeps going on about her rights and how Angeles is a bitch and deserved it and that they should let her back in to give her some more punishment.

I try to slip the bouncers some credits to let us back in but they won't have it. I grab Shana and try to pull her away. She's strong, I always remember she was strong from when we used to play-fight—but not this strong—she's really strong.

I manage to get her away from the bouncers and sit her down on one of the Bent Hill benches—she starts crying and tells me that everything's shit and that she doesn't want to live. I agree with her and comfort her and tell her I know and tell her that things will get better.

She asks me when and I tell her I don't know and that I just have a feeling that one day, someday, hopefully, that things will be better. Shana tells me that she's tried to kill herself five times, that her parents pretend everything's okay, that nothing's wrong, that when they found her swinging from a noose half-dead, they just cut her down and carried on making dinner and left her on the floor half-dead.

She tells me that when she slit her wrists, they visited her in casualty with smiling faces and told her that wasn't it wonderful that her father had been mentioned in the papers and that it was great that Eddy Balls was happy with everything he was doing for the happiness department.

I've heard some of these stories before, some I haven't, but I know what her parents are like and it doesn't shock me. The horrible truth is that even if she killed herself, her parents are so hung up on their work, blind positivity, pills, and happiness that they would've celebrated her death, then gone back to writing speeches, not having lost a wink of sleep.

I tell her that we should get out of here—she asks where and I suggest the Spliff-Tops for a late-night smoke. I tell her that I can score some top-grade skunk (not easy these days). I do so and we drive (even though I'm very drunk) to the Spliff-Tops.

We park up on a deserted stretch that overlooks the beach-huts and pebble-bound coast. It is a beautiful night and the moon is shining intensely.

Shana continues to pour out her troubles as I roll up an old-school carrot joint. A Bavarian guy called Nikolaus showed me how to make this at a summer camp—it's loaded with skunk and should do the trick of blissing Shana out.

I offer her some dog but she declines—smart girl. I'm starting to think that I should really be doing less of the shit too.

We puff away and listen to an old Tricky album through the car's iPalm triplifier.

The bass feels good and the spliff smoke is intensifying the dog. Shana isn't speaking much but she has her hand on my leg—I don't know whether she's conscious of that or not.

I feel like kissing her but that would only be a cliché, so I resist and concentrate on the smoke, the moon, and the music.

2:11 a.m - CHRIS—FELIXSTOWE FERRY

I awake and my first feeling is that I'm cold—the second, that I'm wet. The third—where the fuck am I? And then, what is happening to me?

SEBASTIEN: Do you know why you're here, boy?

CHRIS: No, I don't believe I do.

I can now ascertain that I am in the sea, and that I am tied to something—the new sea breakers maybe? The cold sea is up to my waist and coming up higher—spraying salty and despicably polluted water into my eyes and mouth.

By the light of the moon I can see that several of the bouncers from the Horror Box, including Sebastien, are surrounding me.

SEBASTIEN: You're here, Chris, because you're getting too big for your boots, boy...

CHRIS: Please be more specific?

A sharp crack across the mouth as Sebastien strikes me. My mouth starts bleeding and the crimson blood seeps into the water and seems to complement the sea in a most agreeable fashion.

SEBASTIEN: You've been dealing bad dog, Christopher! You've been selling shit, understrength purple poison that's cut with fucked-up chemicals—making people ill and making my boys look bad.

CHRIS: I don't know what you're talking about, chap. I'm simply a caring conscientious student.

Sebastien cracks me again and takes out a big knife.

SEBASTIEN: You better quit with that bullshit, boy, or I'll cut you up good and proper with my friend Mr. Nasty Knife here.

I bite into the side of my mouth so that I can taste more of the blood against the seawater; the moon looks strangely serene against the clear starless night and the rumbling of the waves is almost romantic. There is a stirring within my underwear as the cold feels hot.

SEBASTIEN: That stepped-on dog shit is making people ill and causing the law, what's left of them, to come down hard on my dealers. You see, we represent certain interested parties that this is causing a concern to.

CHRIS: I believe that *you* would be the interested parties, correct?

SEBASTIEN: Hold his head underwater.

My skull is forced under the water and the freezing cold embraces my forehead. It is hard to see anything in the blackened frigid night waters of the English Channel but I imagine that there are seahorses hopping about in black taxicabs. I can almost taste them.

After what seems like a minute, my head is elevated back to the surface and Sebastien strikes me again—releasing more precious droplets of blood into my taste buds.

SEBASTIEN: Now, we've been watching you—you've got some balls, boy, but you're careless. By selling fucked-up shit, everybody loses. That's why you had to get smacked, that's why you got smacked at New Allenby Park tonight, and that's why you're getting smacked right now.

So the Warthogs did have outside reinforcements at the park tonight? I thought so.

Sebastien strikes me again. If they are foolish enough not to kill me tonight, I'm going to chop up every little one of these chaps, just when they least expect it. Maybe it'll be two days from now or maybe it'll be two years from now, but one thing's for certain—it'll be choppity choppity choppity chop.

SEBASTIEN: If we catch you or any of your gay little hatmen selling bad dog again, you'll end up one hundred miles out in the sea—tied to a fridge-freezer.

I'm already feeling sorry for this individual's lack of intelligence so I don't want to inform him that, technically speaking, one hundred miles out would be France, so I reserve my speech and concentrate on sucking in the blood. A salty gush of seawater forms with a nice globule and is a delight to the senses—like a cup of tea to the brain. This is the last thought I have before I pass out—presumably they put chloroform on me again but I can't tell.

3:39 a.m - SOMEONE SOMEWHERE

My life is a divine nightmare.

4:00 a.m - ANGELES—DREAM

I am flying across the capitals of the world. I have wings like that guy in the garage from that weird book 'Skellig' we read in grade seven. I have a huge net and I'm netting up all the designer clothes from all the designer stores in London, then LA, then New York, then I'm flying across Paris and Milan, Rome and Tokyo—all the time my net is being filled until finally I'm on my way to Moscow and the net is too heavy. I'm weighed down and I have to choose between trying to save my clothes or my life. I can't make a decision—I'm going to die—I wake up with a breathless start before I hit the ground.

5:00 a.m - RUPERT AND SHANA—SPLIFF-TOPS

We must've passed out last night and I awake with Shana in my arms. I take her home, kiss her on the cheek, tell her everything will be all right, and go back to my house for some last-minute revision.

5.30 a.m - VANDERMARK'S ZULU NIGHTMARE DREAM

In the dream I'm in the Zulu War except I'm in school and I'm training up the students to become Red Coat soldiers—and I'm teaching them how to attach old-school compass points to rulers to form an effective bayonet—and now the Zulus are in the school and me and the pupils build defences of tables to keep the Zulus out, and as the Zulus thrust with their spears, the pupils thrust with their pencil bayonets, frantically trying to keep the Zulus out—and it is exhausting—the stress of fighting these hardened determined warriors as I try to keep all the pupils alive so that they can sit their exams—and some of the pupils get injured—and so they're carted off to the corner of a classroom to get better—and now I'm shitting myself because if even one of these kids gets injured—especially in their hand and can't write—they won't be able to sit exams—and that can't happen—and a message comes through the window from the local education authority that unless the Zulus are repelled the students won't be able to sit their exams and I'll be fired—so now I'm frantic!

I grab a ruler, except now it is my sword and I jump up on the table and now I'm like Gordon of Khartoum—battling back the zulus—kicking at their heads and swiping them with my sword—and now due to the ferocity and bravery of my attack, they're retreating—running away as fast as they can—and I'm hot on their heels—chasing them with gusto down the corridors—determined to kick them out for once and for good—and they're dropping their shields and spears everywhere and they can't take it—they're defeated—they're sobbing and running away from me.

Now I'm in a frenzy of terror—like a wild gladiator I am seeing them off—and I throw them out of the school and wag a finger at them—and tell them not to come back—and now I'm closing the door and returning to my soldiers who are all alive and the ones who are injured are patched up so that they can sit their exams—then there is a bang and a shell explodes in the classroom—killing all the pupils—and I look out of the window and there is a Panzer tank in the playground and the head of Ofsted is driving it and he's got a monocle and he's got a big wide smile and he's saying:

'How are all your pupils going to sit their exams if they're all dead, Vandermark!?' And he's laughing maddeningly and now he's firing shells into the school and cackling hysterically, saying, 'How the fuck are you going to repair your school when your budget is so stretched?!' He lets off another shell and says, 'Uh oh, there goes the science lab!'

And now I'm gathering up all the dead pupils and putting them in the exam room and I'm making them hold pens and I'm writing the exams for them and then the head of the local education authority is by my side inspecting all the dead pupils—one by one—checking them for signs of life and saying, 'No, he can't sit an exam. No, this one's dead, too—no, dead, dead, this one's dead as well, another failure, Vandy! Dead, dead, dead, another dead one, what about this one? No, this one's dead. Yup, they're all dead! Oh dear, Mr. Vandermark—due to the poor performance and deadness of your pupils in this year's exams, you're officially fired! And there will be no career advancement and no golden good-bye!'

And I scream out, 'Noooooo!' and then I wake up in a pool of sweat and I'm exhausted and I'm still screaming and I have to phone Mr. Kenworthy to ask if the children are still alive—just to make sure that they haven't been blown up by a Panzer shell or a Zulu attack. I didn't like that dream.

Fortunately, Mr. Kenworthy informs me that the students, as far as he knows, have been completely unfettered by Panzer shelling and there have been no reports of any Zulu incursions into the school. This is most welcome news.

6:00 a.m - WALTHER DANIELS—GULPHER ROAD

It's six o'clock on the morning of the start of my exams and I'm out jogging with my chums from the NYCCC: New Young Conservative Cadet Corps. We're the hope of our generation and of the world at large—we have to remain fit, healthy, and fundamentally strong if we are to steer this glorious nation in the right direction for the foreseeable future.

We in the cadet corps are the muscle. We're the backbone of the New Dawn. If Team Tory needs us, then we will answer the challenge. The BNP, the black militants, the regular militants, the Youth Party—all of these scum will perish at our hands when we get the call.

My five comrades all feel the same way—we are ready to do whatever is necessary to keep England strong and united. Down with the scum—paint the world blue.

We meet at the drill ground three times a week where we practice brain-training, armed and unarmed combat, and political strategy. The other political corps do not have anything as well oiled and prepared as the Young Conservative Cadet Corps—we will prevail.

6:30 a.m - DNA MATLOCK—HOME

I'm checking my Mugbook updates and see someone called Gordon Kasparov has posted up:

'I'm not completely sure but I think I've won.'

'Won what?' I reply.

'Everything...' is Kasparov's retort.

6:56 a.m - MARSHALL—HOME

I wake up and am grateful that I didn't spontaneously combust. It looks like I'll be able to sit my happiness exam after all.

6:57 a.m - CHRIS—FELIXSTOWE FERRY

I wake up down on the beach at Felixstowe Ferry. The Horror Box bouncers must have dragged me up the beach and laid me out—very nice of them and very stupid too—they'll be dead men before the day is through.

I have an instrument saved up for an occasion like this and its use will now be justified by their actions.

But first I take a moment to absorb this beautiful blessing of a June summer's morning: The sun shines delightfully and the sea whispers gently as its mellow waves lap at the pebbles and artificial sand. The sound of the sailboats gently swaying in the water is pleasingly ambient.

Kill them now or take my happiness exam and kill them later? I decide that my exam is an important part of this irony and that I'll take it first and kill them after.

I need a wash so I take off my clothes and bathe in the sea. The water is exquisite: fresh, green, the white fetid foam embracing, the salty deposits divine, and the seahorses that I could not see last night are this morning elegantly progressing up and down, doffing their hats to me as they pass. They are truly regal. It's great to be alive.

7:12 a.m - CYNTHIA CARPATHIAN—BEDROOM

It's 7:12 a.m. and it's the time I dread the most. It's the time when most of the rest of the world gets up—refreshed, renewed, and ready to start the day.

I know this because I researched it. For me, it's the time when I wake up from the very fractured sleep I've had and feel an urgent sense of horror as I realize that I do not have the energy or the willpower to get up.

It's the moment when I usually take another sleeping tablet: a vessel to take me back into my dreams, to get me over this point, to lift me into the post–9:00 a.m. slot when it is already too late to fully engage with this truly horrible world.

8:05 a.m - MICKEY MORRISON—BEATRICE AVENUE

I'm walking to school. I thought I could use the fresh air today—clear my mind and sharpen my perspective. I'm walking along the route I used to take as a kid—all those many years ago—with my friend Chris.

Today it's a warm hazy summer day. The streets are surprisingly quiet. The usual cars come whizzing down Beatrice Avenue on their way out of town to the Ipswich conurbations.

Those damn Ipswich conurbations—my old man keeps going on about the time when he grew up in Felixstowe—saying that Felixstowe was a nice independent town back then—that it had its own council and that there was miles and miles of space between us and Ipswich.

Now it's literally just two miles away. Now you can see the big housing developments being built on the Gulpher estate from my Links Avenue bedroom. It's the same all over the country—the countryside being sacrificed to create budget estates to house a jobless population with no chance of a life. What's the fucking point?

8:07 a.m - CHRIS—SEA WALL

I am walking along the Kingsfleet sea wall on my way to my exam. I managed to blag some breakfast: soyflaps and de-organic orange juice at the Ferry Bistro.

I was offered a lift to the school but this route will give me greater pleasure—this day is too nice to be wasted in an autovehicle.

Along the way I look at the River Deben, the serene summer sky, and the swans eagerly protecting their young, I alternate these visions and thoughts with wickedly cruel and horrible tortures that I plan to inflict on the staff of the Box.

I have a moment of complete affinity with nature and I address the clouds: Ahh, the solitary sanctity of the Suffolk countryside—it doth soothe the soul.

8:20 a.m – CYNTHIA—BEDROOM

I wake up again and everything is dark so I go back to sleep.

8:25 a.m - MARTHA—EMPTY CLASSROOM

I have to sit my exam at 9:00 a.m. so that's why I'm going for a chocolate box break now. I stocked up on the way to school so that I have enough chocolate to last me through the day—I'm even going to take some in with me. Chocolate equals happiness so I should really do well in this exam.

8:30 a.m - RUPERT—SCHOOL FIELD

I'm taking a short break before my exam begins by walking around the school field.

The funny thing is that this field is where we've actually been really happy—playing football at break and lunchtimes—giving each other wedgies—talking about girls and who'd done what. Who'd gone the furthest...Nonsense like that...

When it snowed it was really great—the teachers tried to stop us going outside but we would pile out and then when the dinner ladies tried to call us in we'd besiege them with snowballs.

One of the funniest times was when Mr. Bobbins came out and said in a stern voice, 'Time to come in now, everybody!' There was a moment's pause then everyone just pelted him with snowball after snowball—three dozen must have made impact on his head in a matter of seconds—knocking his glasses off and causing him to reel and stumble—grabbing for the door.

The poor geezer picked up his glasses and scuttled inside—shutting the door firmly behind him to protect him against yet another barrage of snow missiles—banging and sliding down the door. It was great that lunchtime—absolute anarchy. With no teachers or dinner ladies to stop us, we ran riot—we buried kids and made human snowmen out of them—we conducted crazy snowball fights with each other and hassled the local workmen by bombarding them with ice.

After that day of destruction they would lock all the doors to prevent us coming out at lunchtime but we would always have that beautiful lawless day.

That was the day I first Angeles. Most of the girls had gone in but she had stayed out with some of the other girls who were following the sixth formers around. But they kept telling them to fuck off as they were trying to get high in peace so they started to draw their attention to us.

I'd always liked her and so when she asked if I wanted to go behind the scout hut, I said sure. We made out behind there for ten minutes before the bell went—so did a couple of my other friends with some of hers. It felt good with the snow coming down, hitting us gently as we made clumsy attempts to feel each other up.

Her lips tasted of pomegranate—probably because there was a big craze for pomegranate juice at the time—there were little bits of it—the pips that got stuck in my mouth—formed part of our kiss. She was a good kisser too—must've practiced a lot. She tugged at my cock and I had to do everything I could not to come.

I fingered her and she got wet—moaning softly—her labia was quite small—I hear that she's had labioplasty now to make it bigger.

Her ass was small but perfectly formed, tight, and it felt good against the cold of the air. On my right I swear that Mickey Morrison was actually screwing Holly Jessop-Routledge—he would later deny it. And on my left Julian Erickson-Hicks was fingering his girl.

The bell went and we spent a few more minutes indulging then walked our lunchtime dates slowly inside, escorting them to their respective classes.

We never saw those girls again again after that—the grade-fourteen boys finally started to pay them some attention and we were left off the scene. But that will always be a happy day. Maybe I should put that in my exam?

<u>8:31 a.m - HARRISON—SECURE UNIT</u>

Harrison, wearing a straightjacket, is curled up in a ball on the floor.

HARRISON: Blip—blop—blappety blop—blib blab blom—blippity blod blod-rod—sod—fod—skitelly—rickety rop. Rickety top ran doppppppp! Ran! Ran! Ran! Ran! Dopp! Dopp! Dopp!

8:32 a.m - KEVIN—HAMILTON ROAD

I take a quick look at Mugbook and see the usual 'Good luck in your exams' postings. The only one with anything interesting to say is Rudolphio: 'My wanton wastrel ways are getting the better of me.'

I'm heading down Hamilton Road—heading toward the bloody school and the bloody exams. The town is quiet this morning—strangely sedate for this time of the day. I would expect a lot more activity—a lot more people about—maybe they've all disappeared.

I go to turn a corner into St. Andrew's Road when I catch a glimpse of a street news monitor—an advert for Colgate teeth transplants is interrupted by a flashing message that reads: 'God has lost Stan Rusinsky's dog.'

I stop and walk back to get this clear in my head but the message has changed back to the Colgate advert. Must be all that late-night revision messing with my mind.

8:44 a.m - DNA—EXAM HALL

I'm chatting to Mickey Morrison as we wait for the exam to start when Marshall Ryan turns and interrupts us:

MARSHALL: It's ironic really. I'm taking an exam on happiness—a subject I've been studying for years now yet I feel more depressed than I have in years. Something's wrong there.

8:49 a.m - CHRIS—EXAM HALL

I enter the exam hall—still a bit wet from my ferry experience. I look around the hall—approximately thirty of us from my class. The teachers at the front look anxious—they've been up throughout the night with the failing students—drilling and spoon-feeding them the correct answers again and again, and now they hope that they are ready, primed, and able to regurgitate all that drab information.

I don't know who looks more spaced out: the teachers or the overnight pupils at the back. They either overdosed them on caffeine pills and legal learning drugs or didn't give them enough judging from their vacant stares.

I see Angeles has a black eye for some reason.

She smiles at me awkwardly. I smile back and push my arms up in the sky (I don't know why) but she seems to like this, giggling and smiling.

I take my assigned seat to see that my hat is on the table. I turn to Angeles who shrugs. I whisper, 'Thanks,' and she smiles. Now there's chemistry and then there's chemistry. Note to self: after I kill those fuckers I'll definitely have to do something about knowing this girl some more.

At my extreme left is the militant girl. In front of me are the Benidorm twins and by my other side is one of my favourite contemporaries: DNA Matlock.

8:50 a.m - VANDERMARK—EXAM HALL

I'm at the exam hall and I'm losing it. I've been up half the night monitoring and supervising the late-night revision sessions. At this point the exam results could go fifty-fifty.

We're giving the students all the tools they need to pass these exams but really some of them are such empty vessels that whatever you fill them up with just blatantly leaks out. It's hopeless.

*The A** cadre of students are my only real hope—if they are successful, then hopefully that'll be enough of a spearhead to make the authorities happy and keep them off my back for a while. Fuck! Look at Miss Derringer's ass, I'd really like to—*

No! I must control myself...I go to the toilets for a quick two minutes and come back relieved—relieved but still stressed.

Mr. Kenworthy is calling out the register of the examinees.

MR. KENWORTHY: Rusinsky?

RUSINSKY: Here.

Somebody shouts out, 'And how's your dog?' Rusinsky doesn't say anything but looks like he's going to cry.

The chief invigilator is getting the students keyed up while the other teachers go around the hall giving last-minute prep talks and reminders on how to structure their answers.

Mr. Kenworthy is hyping them up by running up and down the aisles pumping his fists.

MR. KENWORTHY: All right, people! Are you ready! Woooooooo! Let me hear you make some noise!!

There is not much response.

MR. KENWORTHY: Come on, people! After all, you're here to do a happiness exam! Now can I hear some happiness please!

It is deathly quiet.

MR. KENWORTHY: I can't hear you, people!? Remember, you can be assessed for happiness in the way you act *now* as well as your exam. Now, can I hear some happiness!?

The hall erupts in a few woops, hollers, and 'yeahs!'

MR. KENWORTHY: That's more like it! Now, a quick reminder, your exam will start in five minutes' time.

Someone shouts out, 'Dickhead!'

MR. KENWORTHY: Who said that?

There's no response.

MR. KENWORTHY: Come on! Who was it?!

Someone shouts out, 'It was your mother, sir!'

8:51 a.m - VANDERMARK—EXAM HALL

I'm going batshit! I'm convulsing with panic and I don't think I can hold onto my mental or physical faculties much longer. I may very well shit myself right here and now. Big creamy lumps of horrific shit invading my trousers and bringing brown horror to the hall. Then it will probably be followed by galloping streams of scared petrified piss.

Where are the five Korean ringers I hired? They're nowhere to be seen and I'm not appreciating this! I'm about to go and murderously head-butt the wall when the first of them comes in, and just as I told him, he goes straight to the seat I showed him on the plan and sits down without drawing attention to himself. I wanted them to be spread apart so it seemed less obvious.

Now the second and third ringers come in together—those dolts, I warned them to come separately.

Well, it's too late to chastise them now—if an inspector comes in (and I've posted lookouts so I'll know), I want everything to appear normal.

But the Korean ringers are good lads and they're just blending in with the others—no one seems to have noticed and my loyal lieutenant, Mr. Kenworthy, is acting cool. He knows the score: his future is riding on this as well.

The fourth comes in, quickly followed by the fifth, not as I'd planned it but at least they're here on time. They will score perfectly and everything will be fine. They're all seated now, everything is falling into place, but oh no! Rupert Richenbach De Hoffman is looking around quizzically at my ringers, he's gesturing to Angeles, whispering something to her, and now Angeles is looking at them snootily.

Mr. Kenworthy quickly interrupts them, 'No talking in the hall.' But Rupert has figured something's wrong. I should quickly go over there and strangle him to death, quickly before he tells the others.

I'll just say it was an accident—I'll just punch him in the head and stomp on his noggin until he's incapable of speech—he'll never have the chance to rumble me.

I'll get Mr. Kenworthy to back me up—everyone will believe me and it'll all be fine—I'll say he started on me, that he was going to kill me, that it's all his fault—but wait! Why is Chris looking at me like that?! He's grinning in that evil knowing way he grins! He knows as well, doesn't he?! Oh shit, oh no! Stop it, Vandy! Get a hold of yourself! Don't shit yourself! Not now anyway! What would the inspector say!?

I'll have to kill him too, I'll kill all of them. If I do that and just leave the five ringers, then my averages will look amazing. Yes, this is a great idea! Fantastic! This is the best plan ever! No! No, it's not a good plan, Vandy! You stupid dumbfuck! You'll ruin your career, you'll forever be castigated as the psycho head-teacher—the mass-murdering demented Deben destroyer!

You'll never be able to explain away killing a hall full of students! It won't hold up in court! No matter how you play it, it's a bad idea, all that hard work will go down the drain, and you'll be finished, finished for good! Never to surface again! My god! I think I'm frothing at the mouth—get a hold of yourself, man! Oh, my god, I think I just felt a stream of scared shit shoot down my inner trouser leg.

<u>8:52 a.m - CHRIS—EXAM HALL</u>

Interesting—there's five new students I've never seen before? I know what's going on here, Vandy, you crafty old devil. Ahh, Mr. Vandermark, you clever conniving chap! Hire some ringer students to bump up the school's averages—very cunning—props for that old man.

I turn to look at him, to give him some acknowledgement for this masterful Machiavellian move but he's frothing at the mouth and looking off into the stratosphere with wide-staring crazy eyes. Nobody else seems to be noticing this but me, but then again, most of these people are selfish callow individuals too caught up in their own morbid self-interest to give anyone else the time of day and certainly not Vandermark—who is barely given one ounce of respect. Poor guy, he may be wrong but I feel somewhat sorry for him. Never knew that I could be so compassionate? What's happening to me?

8:53 a.m - RUPERT—EXAM HALL

What's going on? Who are these new Asian guys? Never seen them before. What are they doing here? I thought I knew everyone in this school. Have I been doing too much dog again? Have these people's faces changed!? I'd heard the corporations were offering neoplastic surgery now—to boost the looks of their walking talking adverts—but I didn't think anyone at this school had qualified.

I whisper to Angeles, 'Who are these new guys? Are they corporate surgery people?' She looks around and I see that she doesn't recognize any of them either—intriguing? Wait a minute…Vandermark is staring at me, and then at the five—what's going on? I go to talk to Angeles again but I'm quickly silenced by Mr. Kenworthy who shouts in my face to be quiet.

8:54 a.m - VANDERMARK—EXAM HALL

Fuck my ghost! It's almost five minutes until the fucking exam starts and there are three empty fucking seats! Who the fucking fuck isn't here!? I pop a Manax and go over to my chief invigilator—we run down the registry list and see that the missing students are Harrison (no chance of him), Anderson Marr, and Rudolphio Match-Rees. If they don't turn up, the results won't look good—especially as these students are potential A** material. I rush outside to see if any of them are with us yet. Sure enough, Marr and someone with a Margaret Thatcher mask are walking in.

The person wearing the Thatcher mask is smoking a cigarette, hobbling, and holding his groin. He takes the mask off and addresses the hall. It's the Match-Rees boy. Thank fuck for that.

RUDOLPHIO MATCH-REES: Now don't you go starting without me now! Sorry I'm late, nob problems!

Behind him, Anderson Marr is slowly sauntering to the entrance. I can't believe this! He has never been late for a lesson in his life—he's always fifteen minutes early.

VANDERMARK: Is everything all right, Mr. Marr? You do realize you have an exam to sit?

MR. MARR: Good morning, Mr. Vandermark, yes, everything's wonderful and thank you, yes, I'm quite aware that I've got an exam to sit—thank you for reminding me.

Marr sits down.

I slow down my breathing and think to myself: two weeks and this will all be over and the summer—the beautiful summer holidays will be upon us—and this will all be behind you, so just hold on, Vandy boy! Don't go mad, Vandy! I am calm for a moment and as I look to the side of the glistening bright sun, at the deep blue sky, I am happy.

Then a crushing thought immediately enters my head and I am reduced to a bumbling mess: 'The darkness is upon you, Vandy-lad! Big gloomy darkness gonna eat you up, boy! Eat you good and proper! No! No! No! Vandy! You won't be able to relax at all—as you've got preparation for the new curriculum to do all summer and on top of that you won't be able to relax as you'll be shitting yourself about the results! So good luck, Vandy boy! You'll be a fucked-up gibbering wreck! Vandy gonna be a mess!'

A sudden surge of overwhelming horror grips me and I feel the urge to run, run out of the exam hall, and run down the street—run at top speed—away forever from this horror—away, faster and faster—away from all this mess—this oxymoron, this pathos, this bathos, this malevolent palpable enmity.

As I run out of the school gates, down the road and into the town, all I hear are negative words, failure words, harmful words, and more destructive defeatist words—gurning and churning again and again in my head—replaying themselves with deafening terror!

My mind is in such a tailspin of horror I almost stride right into a rabid dog that bounds past me in the opposite direction.

8:59 a.m - MR. KENWORTHY—EXAM HALL

MR. KENWORTHY: Right, well, I'm sure Mr. Vandermark wishes you all the very best of luck in your happiness exam and now is indeed the time to start. So, students, if you'd like to open your papers and begin: you have exactly three hours.

Anderson Marr stands up.

ANDERSON: Sir, if I may, sir, there's just one thing I'd like to say before we start...

MR. KENWORTHY: And what's that, Mr. Marr?

ANDERSON: This—

Anderson Marr takes out a small device from his jacket and presses a button and all the digital explosives that he has spent the last week hiding in the exam hall are activated and the hall's wall, ceiling, and floor explode in a huge ball of flames.

The happiness exam papers are mostly disintegrated by the flames but one is blasted out of the hall and floats in the air outside before landing on a tree.

9:00 a.m - CHRIS O'REILLY—EXAM HALL

It appears that one of my hands has been blown off. I can see the rare sight of my exposed and maimed shoulder in all its naked raw beauty...The last thing I think as I lie in the rubble, my body a torn-apart mess, is that I like Angeles, I like her a lot, and I think she likes me, I—

‘So it is with all joy: life’s highest, most splendid moment of enjoyment is accompanied by death.’

Søren Kierkegaard

‘Thanks to Bret Easton Ellis. The best by far.’

17226547R00112

Printed in Great Britain
by Amazon